BEARS' BEDTIME STORYBOOK

BEARS' BEDTIME STORYBOOK

STORIES AND POEMS BY

BRENDA APSLEY

MOIRA BUTTERFIELD

GEOFFREY COWAN

JEAN MCKENZIE

KATE MONTAGNON

SALLY SHERINGHAM

ILLUSTRATED BY
GRAHAM PERCY

OCTOPUS BOOKS

First published in 1987 by
Octopus Books Limited
59 Grosvenor Street
London, W1

Text and illustrations copyright © 1987 Octopus Books Limited

ISBN 0 7064 3012 3

Produced by Mandarin Publishers Limited
22a Westlands Road
Quarry Bay, Hong Kong

Printed in Hong Kong

GOODNIGHT, JAMIE

Jamie Bear was in bed, but he couldn't go to sleep. He tossed and turned, shook his pillow and pulled the blankets under his chin, but still he couldn't sleep. He looked at the clock. It was late.

Jamie's dad crept into his room. 'Not asleep yet?' he whispered.

'No,' said Jamie. 'I can't sleep. I tried counting sheep, but it didn't work.'

Jamie's dad looked out at the inky-black sky. Stars dotted the blackness. 'Why not try counting stars instead?' he said, and crept outside.

Jamie looked at the twinkling, winking stars and began to count.

'One, two,' he counted, and his eyes felt heavy.

'Three, four,' and he yawned a big yawn.

'Five, six,' and his eyes started to close.

'Seven, eight, nine,' Jamie counted. But before he could say 'Ten,' he was fast asleep.

Jamie's dad peeped in. 'Goodnight, Jamie,' he said.

PLAYTIME

I like dressing up,' said Lucy Bear.
'So do I,' agreed Larry Bear.

They were putting on a play and had borrowed a big basket full of costumes. Larry even wore a false beard.

They had invited all their friends to see the play and their best friend, Bruce Bear, was in charge at the door. Soon, every seat was taken.

When Larry and Lucy arrived at the door, Bruce said: 'No more. Sorry. We're full up!'

'It's *Lucy and me*!' said Larry, lowering his beard.

'Sorry,' chuckled Bruce. 'I didn't recognize you both for a moment! Come on in!'

KEEPING WARM

Brr! I'm freezing!' shivered Patrick Bear, one wintry morning. 'I'll light a fire.'

But when he went to the shed, he saw it was empty.

'Oh, no!' groaned Patrick. 'I'll have to find some more firewood.'

So he put on his hat, boots and thickest coat and set off into the forest. Soon, he spotted a long branch that had broken and was lying on the ground.

'I'll drag that home and make a fire with it,' thought Patrick, picking up one end.

It was hard work. Patrick puffed and pulled until, finally, he reached his garden. Then he fetched a saw and cut the branch into smaller pieces.

'Phew! Finished at last!' he gasped, carrying some firewood indoors. 'But I won't light the fire just yet, after all,' he thought. 'Being so busy has warmed me up nicely.'

WINTER BEAR

Later on that winter's day,
When cold winds blew the sun away,
Patrick lit his cosy fire;
Watched the bright flames leaping higher.
Outside, the snow fell soft and white,
Patrick thought: 'A pretty sight!'
As cosy as a bear could be,
Eating toast and sipping tea.

THE SURPRISE PARCEL

I t was Susie's birthday. Her friend Sam arrived with a big parcel wrapped in red paper, tied with a silver ribbon. The parcel was so big Sam could hardly see over it or round it. He set it down. 'Happy birthday, Susie,' he said.

'What is it?' asked Susie.

'Three guesses,' said Sam.

Susie walked round the parcel. It was lumpy and bumpy. 'Is it a big rag doll?' she asked.

'No,' said Sam. 'Guess again.'

Susie took the parcel to see how heavy it was. 'Is it a play house?' she asked.

Sam shook his head. 'No,' he said. 'One guess left.'

Susie felt the parcel carefully. She could feel six long, rounded, bottle shapes and two much smaller round shapes. 'Two balls,' she said, 'and six skittle shapes. That's it — a set of skittles! What a nice surprise parcel.'

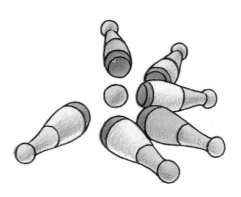

SPLAT!

Young Barnaby Bear decided that
He'd like to be an acrobat.
He juggled with spoons and an ice-cream,
It really was a sight to be seen.
Now Barnaby Bear's decided that
His ice-cream cone looks like a clown's hat!

WHAT'S COOKING?

William was watching his dad cooking. 'What are you making?' he asked.

'Wait and see,' said Dad.

William's dad mixed flour and ginger in a bowl, then he melted sugar, butter and treacle on the stove. He added milk and an egg, and stirred till the mixture was very thick and sticky. 'What can it be?' thought William.

William's dad rolled out the mixture and shaped it. He made fat bodies, arms and legs, then added round ears and currant eyes. William watched and smiled. Now he knew. 'Gingerbread bears!' he said. 'Yummy!'

PATRICK AND THE SNOW BEAR

Patrick looked out of his bedroom window and for a moment thought he had woken up in another land. For the lawn, the flowers, the trees and even his swing had turned a brilliant sparkly white.

'It's been snowing!' he shouted excitedly.

As soon as he had finished breakfast Patrick put on his coat, scarf, bobble hat and boots and ran into the garden. The snow made a lovely crisp crunchy sound underfoot, and he left deep footprints wherever he went. What a pity his two best friends, George and Allen, were in bed with mumps; they could have had such fun tracking one another.

After a while Patrick got bored playing in the snow on his own. It wasn't much fun throwing snowballs when you had no one to throw them at, and what was the point of pretending to be a dragon with white fiery breath if there was no one to watch you? He was beginning to feel a bit lonely.

'I know what I'll do,' he said. 'I'll build a Snow Bear!' and he went to find his father's shovel. For the rest of the morning, he moulded and patted and smoothed and sculpted and shaped. Patrick concentrated so hard he forgot all about being lonely.

At last the Snow Bear was finished. What a work of art!

'Now I've got my very own friend to play with!' laughed Patrick. 'I think I'll call you Snowy.' And even though Snowy was made of snow, Patrick swears to this day that, at that moment, he winked at him.

THIRSTY BEAR

Every Monday, at four o'clock, young Brown Bear visited his Grandma. She always had a cup of tea and made him a jug of hot chocolate to drink. But today young Brown Bear was late and the chocolate was getting cold. Suddenly, young Brown Bear raced in, puffing hard.

'I forgot the time, so I ran all the way,' he gasped. 'Now I'm too hot to drink that chocolate.'

'I guessed you would be,' said Grandma. 'So I added some ice to the jug of hot chocolate. Now you can have a nice *iced*-chocolate drink!'

FLYING!

When I grow up I want to be,
A pilot flying high,
I'll visit foreign countries,
And speed across the sky.
But at the moment I must keep
My feet upon the ground,
I'll fly my model aeroplane,
And watch it zoom around.

THE WALK

Patch the dog lay before the open fire, drowsily dreaming of a big, juicy bone.

'Come on, lazy! You can't just sleep all day,' called Arnold Bear. 'You need some exercise. I'll take you for a walk.'

Patch opened one eye, then closed it again, hoping Arnold would go away. After all, it was very warm and cosy indoors.

But Arnold clipped the leash to Patch's collar.

Patch yawned, stretched and followed Arnold out of the front door.

Outside, Patch sniffed the fresh air. It was full of interesting smells. Patch began to walk—faster and faster. In no time, he was running along, happily chasing leaves and pulling Arnold behind him.

'W . . . wait for me!' puffed Arnold, clinging to Patch's leash.

Later, as they returned home, Patch settled comfortably by the fire once more. So did Arnold.

'You took *me* for a walk!' he gasped wearily. 'Now *I* need a rest, too!'

TED'S SWIM

When Ted woke up and looked through the window the sun was shining and the sea sparkled like diamonds.

'Just right for a swim,' he thought.

He collected his swimsuit and goggles and a beach towel but just as he was ready, a big black rain cloud came over the cliff.

'You'll have to wait until that's passed over,' said his mother.

Ted felt very glum and did not know what to do with himself. Then he had an idea. He took out his easel and crayons and drew a picture of the sun and the sea and the cliffs. But he didn't draw the big black cloud.

By the time he had finished, the rain had gone, the sun was shining and, in two minutes, Ted was happily splashing about in the sea.

The Missing Pancake

Ted was busy making pancakes for supper. First he mixed some flour and eggs in a bowl, then poured the mixture into a pan. After it had cooked on one side Ted threw the pancake up in the air and caught it the other way up. Then he cooked it on the other side. (Only grown-up bears can do this as little bears might get burnt.)

Ted thought that tossing pancakes was great fun. He tossed them higher and higher and at last, one of them didn't come down again. Ted looked up in amazement. There was the pancake, stuck on the lampshade.

He stared in surprise for a minute and suddenly, splosh! down came the pancake right on Ted's head!

Exploring!

Three bears were going exploring.

'It's exciting!' said Martin Bear, packing the kitbag and hamper.

'An adventure!' agreed his brother Malcolm, who was wearing a special explorer's hat and carrying the cooking-pots.

'I wonder what we'll discover?' added their brother Michael. He took a huge kettle so they could boil water over a camp fire.

'Let's explore beyond that hill,' said Malcolm.

They walked quickly at first, but soon slowed down.

'It's hard work,' puffed Michael.

'We've so much to carry,' groaned Martin.

Then it began to rain. In no time, the bears were soaked. So was their food, as the hamper leaked.

'We can't light a camp fire,' shivered Michael. 'Everything's too wet!'

The three brothers hurried home. They felt much better after a steaming bath and supper.

'We didn't discover anything,' grumbled Martin.

'Yes, we did,' grinned Michael. 'We discovered that it's *nicer staying at home!*'

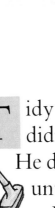

TIDY BEAR

Tidy Bear liked to be busy. So he didn't mind doing the housework. He dusted, brushed and vacuumed, until his home was spotless.

When he had finished, he sat down to rest. But soon he was bored.

'What shall I do now?' he wondered.

Outside, the wind howled. Suddenly, a strong gust blew open Tidy's front door. Dust and leaves swept in from the woods.

'I'll have to clean my house all over again,' he thought, locking the door.

'Oh, well,' he whistled happily, 'it gives me something to do!'

SLEEPY BEAR

After every busy day,
Mother Bear sits sewing,
This time it's a patchwork quilt,
Look how much it's growing!
Every night is just the same,
When we come a-peeping,
Mother's sitting in her chair,
But very soon she's sleeping.
For after all her work is done,
Her children tucked in bed,
Mother Bear is tired too,
See her nodding head!

STANLEY'S TREASURE

S tanley Bear went to the seaside with his parents. While Dad sunbathed and his mother set out the picnic, Stanley pulled on some flippers and a snorkel.

He dived into the sea.

'I'll search for sunken treasure,' he thought.

Suddenly, he saw something on the seabed. Covered with mud, it seemed very old. Quickly, he swam back to the beach, carrying it with him.

'Look! Treasure! Is it gold?' he gasped.

His mother took it and smiled. 'No,' she said, 'and it's quite new, really.'

'How can you tell?' frowned Stanley.

'Because it's the bracelet I lost here, last week,' said his mother happily. 'Thank you for finding it for me.'

ALL FALL DOWN

P icking apples from a tree,
Bertie Bear hummed happily.
But Bertie balanced on a stool,
And he forgot that he might fall!
Sure enough the stool has tipped,
And Bertie to the ground has slipped.
Cheer up, Bertie — look around,
Now all the apples are on the ground!

TERENCE GOES FISHING

For his birthday, Terence was given something he had always wanted — a fishing rod. He hurried to a nearby stream, put his bait on the hook, and waited . . . and waited . . . and waited for the rod to give a little twitch.

'I don't think there can be any fish in the stream,' Terence said to his sister sadly at supper. 'Or if there are, they're certainly keeping well away from me.'

'Don't give up quite yet,' said his sister, smiling to herself, for she had just had an idea.

The next day Terence returned to the stream, put his bait on the hook and waited . . . and waited. At last the rod gave a little twitch. His paws trembled with excitement as he wound up the reel . . . but it wasn't a fish at all but a fish cake!

'Oh, well, I suppose a fish cake is the next best thing to a fish,' said Terence, laughing at his sister's joke!

THE SPECIAL SURPRISE

It was Bessie Bear's birthday. Tom Bear put on his best bow-tie and jacket, and went calling with a present.

'A surprise for you. Happy birthday, Bessie,' he said, when she opened the door.

'Thank you, Tom,' said Bessie. 'I've had such lovely gifts, like chocolates and flowers. I can't think what *you've* brought me!'

'Oh, you've had chocolates already?' asked Tom, looking disappointed. Then he handed Bessie the box which he had gift-wrapped specially.

'It looks beautiful,' said Bessie. 'I wonder what's inside!'

Quickly, she unwrapped the box while Tom watched. But as she lifted the lid, out popped a bright jack-in-the-box.

'Ohhhh!' cried Bessie, looking startled.

'Oh, no!' groaned Tom. 'How did *that* get in there!'

Suddenly, he remembered. Tom's younger brother, Sam, had a box which was just the same size.

'I must have wrapped the *wrong* box, by mistake, before I left home!' he explained to Bessie.

But she just laughed and laughed.

'Why,' smiled Bessie. 'That was the *funniest* birthday surprise I've ever had!'

HELPFUL BEAR

I don't mind helping,
  Really, it's true!
I'll wash up the dishes,
Especially for you.
I'll rinse all the glasses,
Scrub all the pans,
Polish the silver,
With my *bear* hands!
Of course I can do it,
Really, I can,
I'm very helpful,
You know that I am!

TEDDY BUNS

Teddy came home from school all hot and bothered. The sun was burning his fur and he felt like a fried egg. He stamped into the kitchen where his mother was baking.

'Hello,' she said. 'What are you so cross about?'

'I'm too *hot*,' said Teddy in a temper and stamped into the living room. 'What's for tea?' he called out.

'Teddy Buns,' replied his mother.

At tea time, Teddy felt a bit ashamed for being so grumpy.

On his plate his mum had put two lovely spicy toasted buttered *hot cross buns*.

PAINTING IS EASY

One day Annabel Bear watched a television programme called 'Painting made Easy'. Someone showed how to paint large pictures, called murals, on doors and walls. Someone else showed how to make a modern-art picture by splashing different coloured paints on to a piece of paper. Then everyone in the studio tried decorating Easter eggs with bright spots, stripes and squiggles.

'Painting is easy. Anyone can be an artist,' said one of the bears on television. Annabel thought that it looked very easy, too. She decided to try out some of the painting ideas straight away.

Annabel collected all kinds of different coloured paints and some brushes. She started to paint the things in her room.

She painted all the chairs but, because this made them wet, she had to sit on the floor.

She tried painting a big mural picture on the door but, because this made it wet, she couldn't open it!

When Annabel had finished, everything except the television was covered with wet paint.

Annabel sat on the floor and waited for the paint to dry. She decided that being an artist was a very messy job. In fact, she looked like a painting herself, because she was covered in coloured splashes like a modern-art painting.

Annabel decided to write to the bears on television, asking them to make a programme called 'Cleaning up'. And she signed the letter with a paint-covered pawprint.

THE QUARREL

Jake and Penny were always quarrelling. Today they were quarrelling about marbles. 'I'll win all your marbles,' said Jake. 'You'll have none left.'

'No, you won't,' said Penny.
'Yes, I will,' said Jake.
Penny rolled a marble hard. 'I'll win all *your* marbles,' she said.
'Right!' shouted Jake. 'We'll play right now! I'll win, I'll show you.'
Just then their mother arrived. She picked up all the marbles. 'No, you won't,' she said. 'I'm tired of your arguing. The game's over — and so is the quarrel. Come on, it's time to eat.'

BIRTHDAY BEAR

Today is Bertram's birthday,
He's as excited as can be,
With lots and lots of presents,
Now it's his birthday tea!
His friends sing: 'Happy birthday!'
They cheer and jump about,
As Bertram takes a deep breath,
And blows the candles out.
'What a special day,' he says,
'It's one that I adore.
I'm birthday bear. Hooray! Hooray!
Look at me. I'm *four*!'

ROSEMARY'S EXOTIC HAT

Rosemary Bear loved wearing exotic hats covered in ribbons and bows and lace and tassels and frills and net — you name it, Rosemary had worn it!

But now she wanted a particularly exotic one to wear to her daughter's wedding. So she covered her old straw hat with flowers. My, what an exotic hat! The only trouble was, the bees thought so, too. Wherever the hat went, the bees followed.

So Rosemary covered the hat instead with fruit. My, what an exotic hat! The only trouble was, the wasps thought so, too. Wherever the hat went, the wasps followed.

'Oh, dear, what am I going to do?' thought Rosemary. And then she had another idea…

The wedding guests had never seen a hat covered in *vegetables* before! My, what an exotic hat! And what a piece of luck for Rosemary that the caterpillars hadn't spotted it!

BETTY'S BUBBLES

One morning, Betty was clearing out an old cupboard when she found a dirty old clay pipe.

'This could do with a wash,' she said and filled a bowl with water and washing-up liquid and gave the pipe a good scrub.

'But how do I dry *inside* the pipe?' she wondered as she gently blew the water out. To her surprise an enormous bubble came from the other end of the pipe. It sparkled and shone and floated up in the air. Then it popped!

'How lovely,' thought Betty. 'I would like to see another.'

She dipped the pipe into the water and blew gently again. This time, two bubbles came floating up in the air.

Betty forgot all about the cleaning. She sat on the floor with the pipe and her bowl and blew bubbles all morning.

'This is more fun than housework,' said a rather damp but very happy Betty Bear.

DOUGHNUT RINGS

Becky Bear liked playing 'rings',
throwing small hoops over a little peg.
   'Grandpa's coming today,' she thought.
'I'll cook him some doughnut rings, his
favourites.'
   But when Grandpa was late, Becky
went to find him. She saw him on the far
side of the stream between the houses.
   'The bridge is down,' he called,
waving his walking-stick. 'I can't cross the stream.'
   'You can still have your afternoon treat,' said Becky,
and she went to fetch the doughnuts.

'Hold up your walking-stick,' she said.
One by one, she threw the doughnuts
which landed over the end of the
walking-stick.
Grandpa chuckled.
'Just like playing "rings",' smiled
Becky.

SWEET SUSIE

Teddy fell in love,
   With little Susie Bear.
'Soon she will be four,' he said,
'And I'm invited there.
I must take a gift,
Dear me, what shall it be?
I know just the very thing.
Some candies made by me!'

27

THE BEAR FAMILY'S CHRISTMAS

Great Grandfather Bear lived alone in a big old house. He thought Christmas was the best time of the year, a special time when families should be together. So every year the whole Bear family — and it was a big one — travelled from far and near to spend the holiday together at Great Grandfather's house.

Right in the middle of the big old house was a tall hallway. It was here that Great Grandfather Bear put up the biggest Christmas tree you ever saw.

Last Christmas Eve Great Grandfather Bear was still decorating the tree when the rest of the family — aunts and uncles, brothers and sisters, mothers and fathers, nephews and nieces — all went up to bed. 'I'll stay and finish the tree,' he said. 'When it's done I'll know Christmas is really here. You can all come and put your gifts around the tree first thing in the morning.'

Soon the big old house was dark and quiet. William, the youngest great-grandson, lay in his bed and waited and waited. Then he slid out of bed and, still in his pyjamas, crept downstairs. He wanted his presents to be the first ones around the Christmas tree.

What a surprise William got when he opened the door of the big hall! The room was full of aunts and uncles, brothers and sisters, mothers and fathers, nephews and nieces — the whole Bear family! They were still in pyjamas and nightgowns, and they carried gifts of all shapes and sizes.

'I wanted to be the first to put my presents under the tree,' William explained.

'So did we,' said the others. 'Looks like we all had the same idea.'

Great Grandfather Bear hung the last lights on the tree and climbed down the ladder. He looked at his pocket watch. 'It's just past twelve o'clock,' he said. 'Merry Christmas, everyone.'

'Merry Christmas,' said the Bear family. 'Merry Christmas, William.'

A SURPRISE PARTY

The bears were watching a banquet on television.

'I would so love to go out all dressed up and be waited on,' sighed Betty.

Bimbo and Biffy put their heads together, then told Betty to go and dress herself up.

Meanwhile they cleared a space in the outhouse and hung coloured paper round the walls. They made a box into a table and put on it a glass with two straws in. While Bimbo was mixing some fruit juice in a shaker, Biffy put some fruit on a toothpick to make a cocktail decoration. Then they went to fetch Betty. They fussed around her as though they were waiters and Betty sat down at the table, elegantly sipping her special drink.

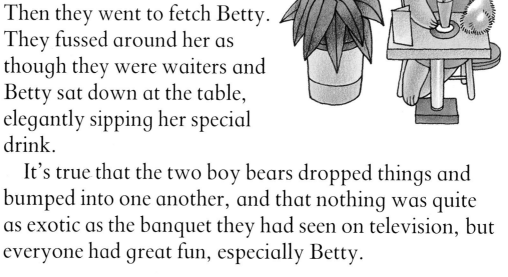

It's true that the two boy bears dropped things and bumped into one another, and that nothing was quite as exotic as the banquet they had seen on television, but everyone had great fun, especially Betty.

PUDDING

Bears love pudding good and hot,
Sweet and sticky in the pot.
It's a favourite thing to eat,
At any meal — a tasty treat.
When Mother Bear calls 'Pudding time',
Her family's waiting in a line,
Table laid — spoons at the ready,
Pudding fit for any Teddy!

THE PICNIC PLACE

One fine day Bright Bear put on her beach robe,
packed a picnic, and went to the seaside.
'I like the sun!' she thought.

Meanwhile, Country Bear put on her hat and walking-shoes and set off for the woods.

'I like the shade!' she thought.

But the beach was too hot and the woods were too cool. Both bears were heading back home, when they met each other.

'I know where we can picnic together!' said Country Bear. Soon, they sat in her garden, which overlooked the sea. There was a big tree beside them.

'We've sunshine *and* shade here!' they smiled.

HUM FOR YOUR SUPPER

Buster and his brothers had a music group and were really rather good. Bruno played the guitar and the others sang. Their favourite place to practise was in the country, so they would often take a basket of food and stay out all day.

One day, they were out practising when the most delicious smell of fried onions and steak floated towards them across the fields.

'Oh my!' said Boris, 'just smell that.'

They could see a car parked by some trees not far away. The lovely smell was coming from near there.

It was a family of bears: Mr and Mrs Bear and their very small twins. The twins could hear Buster and his brothers playing, and wanted to go over to them.

'No,' said Mrs Bear, 'they are big bears. They won't want you.'

Mr Bear was busy with a barbecue, turning the steak over and humming to himself. The charcoal grew hotter and hotter and the smell more and more delicious. The four bears in the field were looking longingly towards the barbecue.

'Do you think they might ask us to supper?' asked Bernard.

'No,' said Buster. 'We can't intrude.'

So, although all the bears wanted to meet each other, it looked as if no one would make the first move. Bruno's tummy started to rumble. His brothers could hear it. They could also hear something else. It was Mr Bear humming as he turned the steaks on the grill.

Softly, Bruno began to strum his guitar in time to the humming; the brothers joined in until they were all humming the same tune as Mr Bear.

'Listen,' said the twins. 'You'll have to talk to them *now*. They're playing for us.'

'All right,' said Mrs Bear, 'run across and ask them to supper.'

The twins scampered across the field and in no time at all the four hungry brothers were tucking into tasty hamburgers.

'This must be what you call humming for your supper,' said Bruno happily, taking another bite.

A BIRTHDAY CAROL

It was a snowy Christmas Eve and the carol singers were visiting all the houses. Nearby, Binkie trudged along in the snow pulling her sledge and thinking about all the others at home getting ready for the Christmas party.

She felt miserable. It was her birthday and with all the fuss about Christmas, nobody seemed to be taking any notice of her. Two tears slid down her face and wet her fur. She wiped them away with her glove and tried to cheer up. She must not spoil the party just because they had all forgotten it was her birthday.

When she arrived home she washed her face and got ready for the party.

It was a lovely party. All the bears were there except the twins.

'Where are Bertie and Brenda?' said Binkie.

'They are out carol singing,' said Tiny Ted, 'and they're going to — Ooops!'

He did not finish what he was going to say because Biffy put a paw over his mouth. Just then, Binkie heard carol singers outside. It was the twins. They were singing a carol she had not heard before.

All the bears stopped talking and looked at her. Tiny Ted's eyes nearly popped out of his head. He couldn't wait any longer.

'It's your birthday carol,' he shouted. 'The twins have written it specially for you.'

> Birthday greetings Binkie Bear
> And love from all we bring you.
> To let you know that we all care
> A special song we sing you.
> Although we've been such busy bears,
> We hope you didn't thinkie
> That we'd forgotten that it was
> The birthday of our Binkie.

Then everyone crowded round Binkie to wish her happy birthday.

'We had to say "thinkie" to make it rhyme with Binkie,' said the twins. 'We hope you liked it.'

'It was perfect,' said Binkie.

PUDDLES

I wonder if, like Patti Bear,
You love puddles, too?
The very deep and muddy ones,
When only boots will do!
For she pretends she's far away,
In the jungle heat,
With fearsome, scaly crocodiles,
Swimming round her feet!
Or, dreamily, she's paddling,
On a desert isle,
In crystal-clear blue waters,
Sand stretching for a mile,
But Patti's in a muddle,
It's plain as plain can be,
She's standing in a puddle,
Nowhere near the sea!

MY FRIEND TED

My best friend is a teddy bear,
Ted's old and worn, but I don't care.
Because, you see, he likes to play
With me at any time of day.
Ted sits beside me at each meal,
He always knows just how I feel.
And when it's time to go to bed,
I always sleep beside old Ted!

A TASTY CAKE

T ed was an untidy cook, and one day he decided to bake a cake.

'This is going to taste really good,' said Ted as he broke some eggs into the bowl. 'Ooops!' he said, as he missed and they fell on the table. What a mess!

The next time he aimed straight and began to beat the mixture.

'Mmm,' he said as he tried some. 'This tastes *really* good.'

He went on adding ingredients then trying a bit more.

'This tastes *really* good,' he kept saying.

He said it so often that when it was time to bake the cake there was none left. He had eaten it all up!

Ted To The Rescue

Ted was a very good swimmer. He could dive from the highest board and stay underwater longer than any other bear. He was the champion at the bears' open-air pool at the seaside.

Sometimes, when he was ready to dive, he would look across at the water-skiers and wish he could have a try. But he had no boat and didn't know anyone he could ask to pull him along.

'Come on Ted, stop day-dreaming,' the other bears would shout, and watch him dive head-first into the water.

Mrs Bear and Belinda came almost every day to watch Ted. Ted thought Belinda looked a lonely little bear. She was very shy and carried a doll with her everywhere she went. Belinda and her mother used to shiver when Ted made his splendid dives. They seemed to think he was very brave.

One day, Ted was paddling in the sea and watching the water-skiers. How he wished he could have a try himself. He saw that Mrs Bear and Belinda were splashing about in the sea. As usual, Belinda had her doll with her.

Suddenly, a huge wave came rolling towards them.

'Look out!' called Ted.

They looked up and began to run back to the shore. The wave seemed to chase them, but Mrs Bear pulled her daughter to safety. In the struggle, the doll was swept out of Belinda's paw.

'Oh my doll, my doll,' cried Belinda, 'save her, somebody.'

She tried to go back into the sea but Mrs Bear held on to her. Ted coolly waded in and swam about until he found the doll. He shook off the water and shyly gave it to Belinda.

'Thank you, thank you,' she said. 'However can we repay you?'

'It was nothing,' grinned Ted. 'Please don't bother about it.'

Belinda whispered something to her mother, and Mrs Bear said, 'We have hired a speedboat for the holiday. Would you like to come for a ride?'

'A speedboat,' said Ted excitedly. 'Oooh, I would love to come water-skiing with you.'

For the rest of the holiday, Ted went water-skiing every day with Mrs Bear, his new friend, Belinda, and, of course, the doll in her dried-out clothes.

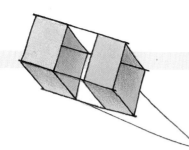

FLYING HIGH

Stanley Bear had two kites.

'I wonder which will fly higher?' he thought, one windy day.

First, he tried his new box-kite. Up and up it soared. Then he flew his old pink and blue kite. It danced and whizzed about, its bright tail flapping in the breeze.

'Hmm,' wondered Stanley. 'It's hard to tell.'

Suddenly the string broke and a strong gust swept away the pink and blue kite, until it was a tiny spot high in the sky.

At last the wind dropped, and so did Stanley's kite.

'No doubt about it now,' grinned Stanley. 'My old kite went the highest!'

WHO'S THERE, BEAR?

When we were in bed, the telephone rang,
It gave us such a terrible fright.
It was Uncle Jim in Australia,
He'd forgotten that here it was night.
'I have just called to say hello,' he said,
'I am sorry the time's not quite right.
I wanted to ask how you're getting on,
I suppose I'd do better to write.'

WILLIAM AND THE APPLES

What was William up to? He was a lazy bear who never did anything for anyone unless there was something in it for him. And now he had offered to spend Saturday picking Winifred Bear's apples for her. And he wasn't just picking the easy ones; he was standing at the top of the ladder and stretching for the high-up ones, too.

'He must be stealing them,' Winifred muttered to herself. But no, his pockets were too small for apples, and there was nowhere else he could hide them.

'You must be turning over a new leaf, William,' she shouted.

William looked down at her and just smiled. He wasn't going to remind her that her garden backed on to the football stadium, and that the reason he was picking apples was so he could have a grandstand view of the match for free!

TED HAS HIS NECK SCRUBBED

When Ted finished his push-ups one day his mother noticed he wasn't wearing the chain he usually had round his neck.

'Was it there when you washed your neck this morning?' she asked.

'Oh, er, I forgot to wash it this morning,' said Ted, and tried to think where he might have lost the chain.

'Go and do your piano practice,' said Mother. 'You haven't done any for a week.'

Ted went over to the piano and there, right on top of the piano stool, was the chain. He showed it to his mother and said, 'It must have been there all week!'

'In that case,' his mother said, 'you can't have washed your neck for a week or you would have noticed you weren't wearing the chain!'

She hauled Ted off to the bathroom and scrubbed his neck clean till it was sore. Poor Ted never forgot to wash it again!

JAKE TAKES A PICTURE

Jessie was a quiet, sweet-tempered little bear, who usually let her brother Jake have all his own way. One day he wanted to take a picture of her for a photographic competition.

'Go and put on some dungarees,' he said.

'No,' said Jessie. 'I'm a pretty bear and I want the picture to show me as I am.'

'It's much better my way,' said Jake.

'I'll do it my way or I won't do it at all,' said Jessie, nicely but firmly. So, for once, Jake had to agree.

This is the picture Jake took. Do you think Jessie was right?

THE BEST BIT OF THE CAKE

Daddy Bear and Thomas were making a fruit cake. They put flour, eggs, spices, sugar and fruit into a big mixing bowl and stirred it with a wooden spoon. Then they baked it in the oven.

When the cake was cooked, Daddy Bear added layers of yellow marzipan, white icing, cream swirls and chocolate shapes.

The cake was finished. 'Which bit do you like best?' asked Daddy. 'The fruit cake, the marzipan, the icing, the cream or the chocolate?'

'None of those things,' said Thomas. 'The bit I like best is licking the spoon.'

BRENDA'S NOTEPAD

Brenda Bear woke up and looked at the notepad by her bed. If there was anything she had to remember, she always wrote it on the pad. CLEAN THE HOUSE, she read. 'Oh,' sighed Brenda, 'I forgot about that.' Brenda wrote another note on the pad, then went to the kitchen.

With mops and buckets, brooms and dusters, Brenda scrubbed and polished and brushed her house all morning. Then she went back to her notepad and read another note. 'Oh,' she thought. 'I forgot about that.'

Brenda put on her beach clothes and went out, carrying her air-bed, snorkel and flippers. She was smiling.

What was written on the notepad? SWIMMING!

THE PUPPET SHOW

I wondered what to do today;
I felt really bored and low.
Then Mother had a good idea:
To put on a puppet show.
The play's about a lady fair
And a pirate — yo, ho, ho!

LEAPFROG

Rachel and Ronald didn't have a garden, so they often played on a patch of earth outside Mrs De Bear's dark, old-fashioned house.

Mrs De Bear dressed all in black and Rachel and Ronald were sure she was a witch.

'Go away, you horrible children,' she would shout, waving her black rolled-up umbrella. 'Go away, and leave me in peace.' Rachel and Ronald always ran off before she could cast a spell on them.

One day Rachel and Ronald were playing happily outside Mrs De Bear's house. They thought she was asleep or out shopping, because she hadn't yet shouted at them. Rachel leapfrogged over Ronald, and went so high that she could see through Mrs De Bear's window. And there she saw the black, rolled-up umbrella waving, but no Mrs De Bear! 'I think she's signalling for help!' said Rachel. 'Come on.'

Now wasn't the time to worry about Mrs De Bear being a witch, about being turned into frogs or put in a pot and boiled up for dinner. This was an emergency! Taking a deep breath, they rushed into the house.

Mrs De Bear was lying on the floor with a broken leg. Rachel and Ronald phoned for an ambulance.

A few days later, Mrs De Bear was back at home with her leg in plaster. 'And to think, my dears, if you hadn't been playing outside I could have lain there for days,' she said, beaming at Rachel and Ronald. 'Now, what can I give you as a reward? Ah! Perhaps you would like to look through my dressing-up box. I used to be an actress, so I have lots of costumes.'

What fun they had trying on all the different clothes. Some were very exotic. They even put on a song-and-dance routine for Mrs De Bear, who cried with laughter. 'My dears, you've brought back such lovely memories of my past. You've made a lonely old bad-tempered bear very happy. You must come and play here whenever you like.' And so they did. It was much more fun than playing leapfrog on the patch of earth.

'And we thought she was a witch!' said Rachel.

'You should never judge a bear by what he wears,' laughed Ronald wearing a wizard's hat, a swirly black cloak and a false moustache.

ODD EGG

M y serve!' said Jake Bear. He was playing table-tennis with his sister, Jessie. Jake hit the ball extra hard. It bounced off the table, past Jessie, and into the kitchen.

Mrs Bear was making a cake. Her electric mixer was noisy, so she did not hear the ball.

'I'll add the last egg to my cake mix now,' she thought, reaching into the open egg-box beside her.

'What a strange egg!' she gasped.

'That's my table-tennis ball,' said Jake, peering round the door. 'Of all the places for it to land.'

'Lucky *I* didn't mistake an egg for our ball,' laughed Jake. 'That would have been messy!'

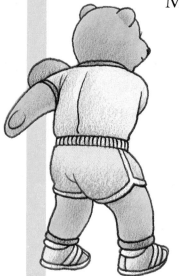

PIRATE PETER

D o come and join our barbecue,'
Says Pirate Peter Bear.
'We've lots of food for you to eat,
And everybody's there!
Hot hamburgers and beefburgers,
And mushrooms on a stick,
Already cooked and sizzling,
Come now and take your pick!
This really is the way to eat,
It's very much more fun,
To have a meal out-of-doors,
While sitting in the sun!'

BLIND BEARS' BUFF

Betty had been trying to give Ted a kiss all Christmas. She knew that if you stand under a piece of mistletoe someone is supposed to kiss you. Betty kept standing under it, but Ted pretended not to notice and took good care not to stand under any mistletoe himself.

Then the time came for Blind Bears' Buff. Ted had a handkerchief tied round his eyes and was trying to catch other bears.

'Now's my chance,' thought Betty.

She stood still under the mistletoe and let Ted catch her. Ted whipped off the hanky to see who he had caught. He was surprised when he saw that *he* was the one who had been caught.

He gave Betty a nice Christmas kiss. The other bears laughed and clapped and, really, Ted didn't seem to mind at all.

COOKERY SCHOOL

Bruno was a greedy bear. He loved food. 'I'm going to cookery school,' he said, 'then I can eat all day long.'

On the first morning Bruno and the other pupils lined up to show the teacher what they were going to cook. The first bear had rice, the second bear cabbages, and the third bear a big pumpkin. Then came Bruno carrying a very heavy basket of potatoes. The other bears had carrots, onions, tomatoes, bottled plums, flour and apples.

All day long the bears peeled and chopped, sliced

and mixed, boiled and baked. Bruno felt very tired.

At the end of a long day the bears lined up again so that the teacher could taste what they had cooked.

One bear carried a stew, another soup, then came fruit, a pink pudding, apple cake, carrot cake, pumpkin pie, plum cake and a casserole. And who was at the end of the line? Bruno, with a heavy bowl of mashed potato.

It was late when he got home. 'What would you like to eat?' asked his mother.

Bruno groaned and pulled a face. 'Ugh!' he said. 'Don't mention food. I never want to eat again!'

FUNNY BEAR

What a funny bear am I,
   In my smart clown's clothes,
I don't need a painted mouth,
   Or a bright-red nose.
For I have some big balloons,
   Come and watch them fly,
Dancing through the air they'll go,
   You'll laugh as they float by!

GUESS WHO?

It was Christmas, and young Brown Bear had been invited to a fancy-dress party.

'H'mm! What can I go as?' he thought.

At last, he had a good idea. 'Of course!' he said, hurrying off to find his mother. Soon, she helped him to make a bright red suit, a cap with a white bobble on top, and a woolly beard to wear round his chin.

When he arrived at the party, his friend came to the door, and said: 'I know who you're meant to be... you're Santa Claus!'

'Not quite,' laughed young Brown Bear. 'I'm Santa *Paws*!'

GARDENER FRED

Fred Bear lived in a big city, but his favourite pastime was walking in the local park. He loved to see the bright flowers, the leafy bushes and the neat green grass. In fact, he thought he would like to be a gardener very much.

But Fred didn't have a garden of his own. His home was three floors up from the ground. So Fred made himself a windowbox, which he hung outside his bedroom window. He filled it with as many plants as he could. He learnt which were the best ones to grow, and when to water and feed them. After a while he became quite a gardening expert.

Soon there was no more room in Fred's windowbox for any more plants. So he went back to the park, and told the park-keeper all that he had learnt. The park-keeper was very impressed, and asked Fred if he'd like to become a gardener. So now when Fred walks through the park he is usually mowing the neat green grass, and all the flowers and bushes he sees, he has grown himself!

THE AFTER-CHRISTMAS PARTY

When it gets cold, bears get sleepy. Sometimes in the winter they sleep for days and days.

One snowy December, Small Bear slept for a whole week. The only trouble was — he missed Christmas! When he woke up he was very unhappy.

'No presents!' he thought sadly, 'and I've missed the Bears' Party at Big's. What am I going to do with all the cakes I made?'

Just then the telephone rang. It was Big.

'Have you been asleep, Small?' he asked.

'Yes,' said Small. 'I'm sorry I missed the party.'

'You haven't!' boomed Big. 'I was asleep, too, and so was everyone else. We're having the party today instead. Can you come?'

'Yes, please!' shouted Small.

He packed the cakes on to his sledge and set off.

It was the best Christmas party the bears had ever had — even if it was three days late!

Mr Simpkins's Christmas

Everything other bears love about Christmas, Mr Simpkins hated. He didn't like turkey, presents, carols, holly, crackers or paper hats. His idea of a perfect Christmas was sitting in his favourite armchair, eating a hamburger and watching television on his own. Although he was always pleased to see his grandchildren, Kate and Joe, at Christmas he really preferred a quiet life.

One particular Christmas seemed worse than ever. The crackers were noisier, his grandchildren were naughtier, the turkey took hours to cook and the plum pudding caught fire! Kate banged her new drum until she grew bored with it and Joe sulked because he hadn't been given a Superbear outfit. Poor Mr Simpkins went to rest in his favourite armchair.

Straight away Mr Simpkins jumped up again like a jack-in-the-box. Someone had left a piece of holly in his favourite chair! He looked cross for a moment and then saw that Kate and Joe were laughing at their practical joke. Mr Simpkins had to laugh too — imagine being caught out by such a simple trick! At last everyone felt in the party mood, so they spent the rest of Christmas playing all kinds of tricks and games.

Perhaps Christmas wasn't so bad after all!

DIY TED

The bears were going camping.

'I'm not sleeping in a leaky tent!' said Ted.

So he bought a ready-made little wooden shed and took it with him in his van.

Biffy and Bimbo thought this was very funny. When they had pitched their tent they went off to enjoy themselves, leaving Ted to mend some loose boards in the shed. He was just hammering in the last nail when they came back, still laughing.

When it got dark, the bears all went off to bed. Biffy and Bimbo were still laughing at Ted as they crawled into their little tent.

But in the middle of the night there was a terrible storm and the rain poured and poured. Soon it began to leak through the tent, and dripped on to Biffy and Bimbo. They got so wet that Ted let them shelter in his dry wooden shed.

'Who's laughing now?' Ted said.

FEED THE BIRDS

Do you like to feed the birds,
  Just like Bernice Bear?
Can you see them by her boots?
How many birds are there?
When they all fly down to her,
She says, 'Come and see,
I've breadcrumbs from my breakfast,
And cake crumbs saved from tea!'

FEELING HUNGRY

It was a cold day. Bernice Bear peered out of the window and saw lots of birds sitting about. They had fluffed out their feathers to keep warm and they didn't look very happy.

'They look hungry,' thought Bernice. So she put on her hat and went to buy some wild-bird seed.

It was quite a long walk home. But when Bernice got back, the birds were still there. She changed into her boots, as the garden was very wet.

'Here you are,' she called, sprinkling seed on to the grass. The birds swooped down and ate it.

Then Bernice walked into the woods and threw down more food for the birds there.

'That was hungry work,' she thought, as she left. 'I've fed the birds. Now I'll feed me!'

SUSAN'S BIRTHDAY

Susan woke with a feeling in her tummy; the sort of feeling when you know today is different from other days. And then she remembered. It was her birthday! She got up and crept into the dining-room to look at her presents. But where were they? She looked in the sitting-room and the kitchen and even the garage. Not a sniff of a present! 'They must have forgotten it's my birthday,' thought Susan.

After breakfast, her mother said they were going to Granny's.

'I don't want to go,' said Susan sulkily, but eventually her mother managed to persuade her. And there, on Granny's dining-room table, was the biggest, most inviting-looking pile of presents Susan had ever seen!

'Bet you thought we'd forgotten your birthday,' laughed her brother Jim.

Susan was already busy opening her surprise birthday presents, so she just answered with a very happy smile.

TEDDY BEARS' PICNIC

Sally and Ian had won a singing competition. As a reward Mr Jones, their music teacher, took them for a picnic. But they weren't getting on very fast. Every time Mr Jones saw something that reminded him of a song, he would play it on his guitar and Sally and Ian would have to sing. When they walked up a hill he played *Jack and Jill*, when they passed some sheep he played *Little Bo-Peep* and when they passed a well he played *Ding Dong Bell*. It was nearly dark when, at last, they got to the picnic spot, and Ian and Sally were famished.

'Now, children, we'll have one more song before we eat,' said Mr Jones. Sally nearly said, 'We have to sing for our supper, do we?' but managed to stop herself, because Mr Jones would have made them sing *Little Tommy Tucker*!

I expect you can guess what they did sing. Yes, it was the *Teddy Bears' Picnic*! At last!

THE DISAPPEARING CAKE

The bears were enjoying Biffy's birthday party when, suddenly, the lights went out. When they came on again, one of the cakes had disappeared. Someone had hidden it.

'It wasn't me,' said Barbara. 'I was giving Bertie some potato salad when the lights went out.'

'And I was pouring out some orange juice for Betty,' said Bernard.

'I was talking to Bertie,' said Boris.

'I was putting ketchup on my hamburger,' said Billy.

'I was just going to eat some cake,' said Bertram.

'I was sitting with my balloon, thinking what a nice

party it was,' said Bimbo sadly.

All the bears were making such a noise that Binkie could not explain that *she* knew where the cake was!

At last all the bears stopped talking.

'I know who took the cake,' said Binkie, finally. 'It was Biffy!'

'Oh dear,' said Biffy, turning quite pink.

All the bears looked at him with curiosity.

'I'm sorry,' he said. 'It is my favourite, chocolate cake, and I wanted to eat it all by myself!' Without anyone noticing, he had switched out the lights, so that he could hide it.

'I'm sorry for being so greedy. I won't do it again,' said Biffy — as he cut a big slice of cake for everyone.

ROBERT BEAR GOES ON HOLIDAY

Robert Bear was going on holiday. He packed his big bag carefully and was going to close it when he said, 'Have I packed my toothbrush?' He couldn't remember, so he unpacked the bag. Out came shorts and jeans, sunglasses and shoes until — right at the bottom — he found his toothbrush.

Robert packed his bag again, then said, 'Did I pack my swimsuit?' Out came coats and shirts, socks and hankies until — right at the bottom — he found his swimsuit.

Robert closed the bag. 'Phew,' he said. 'After all that I *need* a holiday.' And off he went.

TEDDY'S TUMMY ACHE

Teddy said, 'I'm feeling quite funny.
I've got a pain inside my tummy.'
The doctor looked at Teddy in bed,
And when he'd seen him quietly said,
'I know why you've got a tummy ache —
It's a simple case of TOO MUCH CAKE!'

THE OLD TRUNK

I t's too cold to play outside today,' said Bertie Bear. 'There's snow everywhere, the pond is covered in ice, and I've got nothing to do.'

'Come and help me,' said his mother. 'I'm busy emptying this old trunk.'

Bertie watched as his mother opened the trunk. She pulled out a big straw hat, a lamp, and lots of dusty books. Then Bertie spotted something much more interesting. 'Whose are these?' he asked as he pulled out some old ice-skates.

'They belonged to your father when he was young,' said Bertie's mother. Then she smiled at him and asked, 'Are you thinking what I'm thinking?'

Bertie smiled back. 'Yes,' he said. 'Now I'm glad the pond is frozen — because I'm going ice-skating!'

And that's just what he did!

WISE OLD WILLIAM

William, Lucy and James had been out shopping, and on the way home Lucy went into a bric-a-brac store. She looked around for so long that William was afraid they would miss the bus.

'We've plenty of time,' said Lucy. She had her eye on an enormous striped umbrella, but when she finally decided to buy it the bus had gone.

'See what you've done!' said James crossly as they started walking home.

They were almost home when it suddenly began to rain. Lucy whipped open the umbrella and they all sat under it until the shower had passed.

'There you are,' said Lucy triumphantly. 'Aren't you glad I bought it?'

William thought to himself, 'If she hadn't made us miss the bus we would have been home before it rained.' But he knew that sometimes, for the sake of peace, it is a wise thing for a bear not to say what a bear is thinking!

LOST IN THE WOODS

Bimbo and Biffy were off for a day in the woods. They hadn't gone far when Bimbo's lunch-box flew open and out fell all his food.

'I told you to have the catch mended,' said Biffy crossly. 'You'll have to share my food now.'

The bears enjoyed their day out (except they were both a bit hungry). But when it was time to go home they could not find the way.

'I think it's this path,' said Biffy.

'No, I think it's this one,' said Bimbo.

'We seem to be lost,' said Biffy in a very small voice.

Suddenly, Bimbo saw something lying on a different path altogether. It was part of the lunch he had dropped.

'Biffy,' he cried, 'this is the way we came.'

So the bears took that path and were soon safely back home.

Before the bears next went out for the day, Bimbo mended his lunch-box and Biffy bought a map showing *all* the paths through the woods.

THE SECRET PLAN

It was very early in the morning. Thomas Bear shook his father awake. 'Wake up,' he whispered.

'What is it?' said Father, still half asleep.

'Ssssh,' said Thomas. 'Have you forgotten our secret plan?'

Father smiled. 'I remember now,' he said. 'Come on.'

Together they tiptoed to the kitchen. Father boiled an egg and made some tea, and Thomas carefully buttered some toast. Father laid a tray, and Thomas added a tiny vase with a flower in it. Then he added a white envelope with MOTHER written on it.

They crept quietly into the bedroom. Thomas's mother was still sleeping. Thomas shook her gently till she opened her eyes and smiled. 'What's this?' she said when she saw the tray Father was carrying.

'It's our secret plan,' said Thomas. 'Breakfast in bed. Happy Mother's Day!'

BATHTIME

When Barnaby Bear took a bath
It used to make him cry,
For when he had to wash his fur,
The soap got in his eye!

But now he finds his daily wash
A much more pleasant task,
Since his dad has lent him
His great big snorkelling mask!

THE MOUNTAIN

James and Tim set off to climb a high mountain one day. James carried a huge rucksack on his back.

'What's inside?' asked Tim.

'Wait and see,' said James.

They climbed up, up, up, up, until they got right to the top of the mountain. It was very high, and they could see for miles.

Tim took sandwiches and fruit from his rucksack, but when James opened his, he took out — a camera and a tripod!

'I'm going to take a photograph to remind us of the day we climbed the mountain,' said James. 'Smile please!'

STEPPING STONES

I bet I can run along that path without stepping off the paving stones!' said Jessie Bear to her brother, Jake, as they played in the park.

'I bet I can, too!' replied Jake.

They like to have competitions.

Jessie went first. But she wobbled on one foot and landed on the grass. Then Jake had a go. He soon trod on the grass, as well. So they went to try again.

Suddenly they saw a huge, strange face behind them. They didn't realize it was only a fancy-dress mask.

'Run!' shouted Jake.

They raced along the path together, leaping from one stone to the next.

'It's only me!' called their friend, Patrick Bear. 'I wanted to show you this mask I made.'

Jessie and Jake laughed.

'At least we didn't step off the path that time,' said Jake.

PATRICK'S PUMPKIN

Patrick Bear grew a pumpkin. It was so heavy, he could hardly carry it. So he pushed it along in his wheelbarrow.

It was so big, it won first prize at the pumpkin show. Patrick felt very proud.

Soon, lots of friends came to see his famous pumpkin.

'You're so clever to have grown it!' said one visitor.

'It's enormous!' added another.

'What will you do with it?' asked a third bear.

Patrick glanced around the crowded room, then had an idea.

'I'll show you!' he grinned. 'Come back tomorrow.'

By the next day he had baked the biggest pumpkin pie his friends had ever seen. Patrick gave them all a large slice.

'This is the best way for everyone to enjoy my pumpkin!' he laughed.

His friends agreed.
'It's *delicious!*'

JANE'S PRESENT

Mrs Jane Bear stood at the sink. A tear splashed into the washing-up water. It was her birthday, and she had set her heart on a shiny red handbag. But what had her husband Jim given her? A feather duster! Jim often liked to tease Jane, but she didn't think this was very funny.

'He can't love me any more,' she thought sadly. 'For you would never give someone you love a feather duster.' And another tear plopped into the water.

'Hello, darling,' said a voice behind her. It was Jim, with a flower in his buttonhole and a present under each arm. 'The feather duster was just a joke,' he said. 'Here are your proper presents.'

One was Jane's favourite perfume and the other was . . . yes, the shiny red handbag.

What a happy birthday it had turned out to be!

Ben Goes Camping

Ben was going camping for the very first time. He pitched his tent at the edge of a wood. He felt rather nervous. It was very dark and very cold, and there were sinister rustling sounds coming from the wood — who knew what was lurking there? Just say a ferocious wolf were to gobble him up in the night, or a ravenous bird were to peck off his nose, or a fierce...

'Don't be such a baby,' said Ben out loud. 'As soon as I light the camp fire I shall be quite safe. Wild animals are afraid of fire.'

Once the cheerful flames started to crackle and flicker, Ben felt much happier. He hung a pot of baked beans over the fire, held out his paws to warm them, and whistled to drown any rustling noises.

'Maybe camping isn't so bad after all,' he laughed. 'In fact I could even get to like the outdoor life!'

GETTING THE BETTER OF BUSTER

Buster was a very large bear with an appetite to match. But Ted thought he was just greedy. One day, to make him look silly, Ted baked an enormous burger bun, filled it, and took it round to Buster's house.

A crowd of bears followed him and saw Buster come out to meet Ted.

'I've brought you a little snack,' said Ted cheekily.

'Thanks,' said Buster. A grin came over his face as he felt the bun. It was as hard as iron. 'Just what I've been looking for. The door of my shed is sticking.'

Buster held the long bun under his arm and ran for the door. He rammed the bun against it and it burst open. How the bears laughed. Every time they saw Ted afterwards they called, 'Baked any good buns lately?' He never tried to get the better of Buster again.

A PRIVATE MUNCH

I t's great to sit out in the garden
Enjoying a private munch,
But it bothers a guy
When a passing fly
Brings four of his friends to lunch.

MEALS ON WHEELS

B arrie Bear was ill in bed, so Auntie Bear decided to take something to eat round to his house. But when everything was ready the car would not start.

'Bother!' said Auntie Bear. 'I'll have to carry the food there instead.' Then she had a clever idea . . .

Auntie Bear put all the dishes on to a trolley and she began to push it along the lane. All the time she kept a sharp lookout for anything coming up behind her.

When she came to the crossroads the policebear held up the traffic for her.

Barrie was delighted with his surprise meal. And when he was better, he bought Auntie Bear a hooter for her trolley.

73

THE CRAFTY COOK

Pierre Bear, the famous chef, held a cookery class one day. 'I'm going to ask you a question,' he said to his pupils. 'Anyone who gets the answer wrong will have to wash the dishes at the end of the class. The question is…how do you make a milkshake?'

The first young bear didn't know. He could only make chocolate buns.

The second young bear didn't know. He could only make strawberry jelly.

The third young bear didn't know. He could only make gingerbread bears.

But the fourth young bear put his paw up, because he knew. 'The way to make a milkshake,' he said, 'is to creep up behind it and shout BOO!' And for that awful joke Pierre Bear awarded the fourth young bear the prize of . . . washing the dishes!

THE TREASURE HUNT

One day three teddy bears found an old map, with a large black X marked on it. They couldn't read the words on the map, but they decided that it said: 'Treasure hidden here.' They guessed that the X marked where a pile of gold and silver was buried.

So the bears decided to go on a treasure hunt. They thought it might be a very long journey, so they took some supplies to keep them going — a bottle of orange juice, a box of sandwiches and several jars of honey.

This was just as well, because the words on the map actually said: 'Good picnic site'. When the bears reached the place marked on the map, they searched high and low, but they didn't find treasure hidden anywhere. So they had a delicious picnic instead, and took home only a pile of empty honey jars.

THE MAGIC EGGS

The Wise Old Bear of the Woods was sitting dozing by the side of a footpath. Next to her was a basket of eggs. Along came Sam and Jenny all set for mischief.

'Look,' whispered Sam. 'Let's play a game with these eggs.'

'Oh, come away,' said Jenny. 'They might be magic eggs, and the old bear might put a spell on you.'

Sam just laughed and quietly took the eggs from the basket. Still the Wise Old Bear slept on. Sam and Jenny began to play a game with the eggs, rolling one along the ground and trying to hit the others with it.

Soon the Wise Old Bear woke up. She opened one eye and looked at the two bears playing with the eggs. She said nothing, but smiled slyly to herself.

'Listen,' said Jenny after a minute. 'What's that?'

Sam listened. He heard a 'cheep cheep' noise coming from inside each egg. Then he heard a pecking and a cracking and the eggs started to open. Out of them hatched yellow chicks which ran all over the place.

Up jumped the Wise Old Bear.

'What have you done to my eggs?' she cried. 'Catch those chicks at once!'

It took Sam and Jenny a long time to catch all the chicks, and then they said they were sorry for being so naughty. Afterwards they often wondered if the Wise Old Bear had known that the chicks would hatch just then, or if her eggs really were magic.

BEDTIME BEARS

When a bear can hear rain
On the window pane
And the night wind moans and wails,
Any sensible Ted
Will trot off to bed
With some books of fairy tales.

THE NEW YEAR SWEATER

Bimbo wanted to knit Biffy a warm sweater. He wanted it to say 'Happy New Year', as Biffy would be wearing the sweater during the cold month of January.

When the time came to wind the wool, Biffy helped Bimbo. There seemed to be rather a lot of wool.

'Do you really need all this?' asked Biffy.

'Oh yes,' said Bimbo, 'I'll make it big, in case it shrinks in the wash.'

On the cold winter evenings the friends sat happily together by the fire, talking about old times while Bimbo's needles clicked. Biffy often looked at the sweater, which was growing longer and longer. 'I'm sure it's going to be too big,' he thought.

On New Year's morning Bimbo gave Biffy the parcel. Biffy opened it as though he had never seen the sweater before. It was ENORMOUS!

'Put it on,' said Bimbo excitedly. Biffy pulled it over his head and stood there with a bright smile on his face.

'It's great, Bimbo,' he said.

Bimbo looked very anxious. 'Are you sure? It looks a bit big,' he said.

'Oh no,' said Biffy. 'It's fine. I expect I'll grow into it.'

He tried hard to look as though it fitted him, but the
sleeves dangled over his paws and the sweater was
nearly long enough to trip him up.

Biffy looked at his friend for a minute and then
began to laugh. He laughed and laughed until he was
almost crying.

'Oh dear,' said Bimbo, wiping his eyes. 'You were
only saying it fitted to please me, weren't you?'

'Well, yes,' admitted Biffy.

'You can't wear it like that,' laughed Bimbo. 'But
I've got an idea. I'll sew some buttons along the bottom
and you can use it as a sleeping bag on these cold
winter nights!'

THE TOUGHEST COWBOY IN THE WORLD

T he world's toughest cowboy sat in the rocking chair eating his hash. He was thinking about all the wonderful things he had done that day. He thought of the cattle he had rounded up and the rustlers he had caught. He thought of the outlaws he had chased across the prairies.

He was just thinking about the oil he had struck on his land when his mother came in with his second helping of hash.

'Ted!' she cried. 'Get out of your father's chair at once. And take your hat off in the house *and* get your feet off the stove. Whatever were you thinking about?'

'Nothing, Ma,' said the toughest cowboy in the world. 'I was just pretending.'

A SKATING SURPRISE

Brian Bear went to his local ice rink to learn how to skate. He stepped carefully on to the ice, where lots of other bears were already gliding around gracefully in time to music.

But Brian couldn't glide at all. In fact, he couldn't stop himself slipping and sliding. He waved his paws in the air and kept wobbling backwards instead of moving forwards.

When Brian finally managed to reach the other side of the rink he was very surprised to find that all the other bears were watching him and clapping. Then the ice rink manager came over and awarded him a silver cup, which had 'Best disco ice dancer' written on it.

After his big triumph Brian gave a TV interview. He said that he had decided to give up ice-skating to give other bear skaters a chance.

'A chance to win the cup?' said the interviewer.

'No, a chance to get around safely!' said Brian, giving the cameras a big wink.

KEEP-FIT BEARS

Jake Bear and his sister, Jessie, were out walking when they saw a big sign. 'Bears' Running Race — tomorrow afternoon', it read.

'I could win that!' boasted Jake.

'So could I!' insisted Jessie.

So, next morning, they decided to do some exercises to get fit.

'I can do push-ups,' bragged Jake, lying on the ground and pushing himself up by his arms.

'So can I!' said his sister, copying him. 'I can skip for ages, too!' she added.

'Easy!' grinned Jake, borrowing her skipping-rope.

It was very hot. Soon, they both felt tired, and sat down in the shade of a tree...

'Wake up!' said Jake, some time later.

'What's wrong?' asked Jessie.

'Neither of us can win the race now,' said Jake. 'We've both slept right through it!'

STORY BEAR

No matter how I really try,
I can't think what to write.
I put my pen to paper,
And think with all my might!
It really is the silliest thing,
The words are in my head!
But when I go to write them down,
Somehow, I find they've fled!

Jake Goes Fishing

W hat are you doing?' asked Jessie.

'What does it look as though I'm doing?' said Jake. 'I'm fishing.'

'You're not very good at it are you?' she said.

This was true. Jake kept catching his hook on his jacket and slipping down in the water. He was so bad that the fish kept poking their heads up and laughing at him.

At last, one came too near and Jake caught it in his net. It wriggled and squirmed about and he couldn't hold it.

'Help me,' he said, holding out the net to Jessie. She took hold of the fish in her paws. It stopped wriggling and looked at them with sad, fishy eyes.

'I don't think he likes being out of the water,' said Jessie.

'I don't think he does either,' said Jake. 'Let's put him back.'

So they did, and after that the fish sometimes let themselves get caught in the net, just for fun, because they knew that Jake would always let them go again.

THE APPLE TREE

Not very many people know,
That bears love trees, but it is so!
That's why I'm planting one for me,
My very own, *my* apple tree!
Next time, when you are passing by,
Perhaps you'll stop — perhaps you'll cry,
'Look at that tree — Bear's very own!
Can you see how much it's grown?'

BASIL'S BATON

Basil went to watch an orchestra play. The conductor waved a stick.

'It's called a *baton*,' explained his dad.

'What an odd word,' thought Basil.

Later, at home, he put on a record and held up a piece of wood. As the music boomed, Basil waved his home-made baton about, swinging his arms wildly, just like the real conductor had done.

Next moment, there was a crash. Basil had knocked a plant-pot on to the floor.

'Oh, no! I hit it with my baton,' he groaned. 'It should be called my *bat*!'

CHILLY COOK

Yan is an eskimo bear, who lives far away on an iceberg near the North Pole. It is one of the coldest parts of the world, but Yan doesn't mind the cold — he loves it!

All eskimo bears have one problem. They live in igloos made of ice, which makes cooking very difficult indeed. If you live in an ice room, you can't bake a cake, fry an egg or even make a simple slice of toast without melting part of your house!

Yan thought long and hard about this problem, because his hobby is cooking. And, at last, he came up with a great idea. Now he can make his favourite food every day, but he still doesn't bake cakes, fry eggs or make toast. Instead he has become the best ice-cream cook in the world!

THE BED-BOAT!

A...a...atchoo!' sneezed Little Brown Bear.
'Oh, no!' he groaned, wiping his nose. 'I've caught a cold.'

'You must go to bed then,' said his mother.

Little Brown Bear sighed. 'Staying in bed is boring!'

But, later, as he lay there he thought of a good game. He imagined his bed was a boat, and the rest of the room was open sea.

'A storm is blowing,' thought Little Brown Bear, 'and my boat is tossing to and fro!'

He bounced and rocked about so much that he fell out of bed with a thud!

The noise brought his mother.

'What a mess you've made!' she scolded as Little Brown Bear sat on the floor with the sheets all around him.

'You had better come downstairs and sit quietly by the fire,' frowned Mum.

'Pity!' thought Little Brown Bear with a grin. 'I'd rather stay in bed, after all!'

BATHTIME BEAR

Young Bertram Bear hated Mondays,
He didn't think they were fun-days.
His mother really had to laugh,
'And all because you hate to bath!'

'You surely are a silly bear,
Look in the mirror, over there,
Your fur is in a dreadful mess,
After a bath, you'll look your best!'

So Bertram looked and sure enough,
His fur was full of leaves and stuff,
'All right,' he said, 'if you think so,
I'll scrub myself from top to toe!'

His mother was amazed at him,
For he had soap from toes to chin.
He had to say, when dry and clean,
He was the smartest bear he'd seen.

FORGETFUL TED

I've made quite sure the oven's hot
And measured out the honey,
I've warmed it in a little pot
To make it nice and runny.
But I am a forgetful Ted
And all this care I'm taking,
Has sent the thought clean from my head —
I can't think *what* I'm making.

GRANNY BEAR'S RIDE HOME

Bimbo and Biffy were collecting wood for a bonfire, but all they had on their little cart was an old armchair.

'That's not much use,' said Bimbo.

Just then they saw old Granny Bear with her shopping. She looked very tired.

'Can we carry your shopping?' asked Biffy politely.

'You can carry *me* if you like,' said old Granny Bear and climbed into the chair! The bears pulled her home, and when they arrived she gave them a bundle of firewood out of the shed for their bonfire.

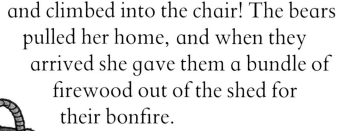

'That old chair came in useful, after all,' said Bimbo.

THE BALL OF WOOL

Lucy Bear was sad. No other little bears lived near her house, so she had no one to play with. She felt lonely.

She looked around for something to do — and saw a long piece of red wool on the ground. She picked it up. 'I wonder where it leads to?' she said, and decided to find out.

Lucy followed the red wool as it zig-zagged through the long grass and across the path. Then she followed it round the big tree and under the bushes.

Lucy was so busy following the red wool that she almost bumped into a little bear standing by a gate.

'You found my wool,' said the bear. 'It rolled away when I was unpacking. I'm Ben, and I've just come to live here.'

'Oh, good,' said Lucy. 'Now I'll have a friend to play with.'

'And so will I,' said Ben.

A Fur-coloured Door

Jessie and Jake were painting their front door. They had decided to paint it the same colour as their fur, so that it wouldn't show if they splashed themselves. But they had no brown paint.

'What colours have we got?' asked Jessie.

'Red, yellow and blue,' said Jake.

'Well, mix them together,' said Jessie.

Jake set to work. He painted part of the door red, part yellow and part blue. When Jessie saw it, she laughed.

'You silly bear,' she said. 'I meant, mix them in the pot.'

Jake felt very foolish. He mixed some red and yellow and blue paint in a spare pot, and the three colours together made brown.

After they had stirred the paint well, Jessie and Jake painted the door and by the end of the day it was a lovely fur colour.

'*And* you can't see where we have splashed ourselves,' said Jake happily.

WINDY DAY

I t was a windy day.

'Good,' thought Big Bear. 'I'll wash my track suit. The wind will dry it nicely.'

But the washing-machine was too hot and the track suit shrank.

'I'll never get into *that*,' thought Big. 'Still, I may as well hang it out to dry.'

That afternoon Big was fetching his track suit off the line when he saw Small Bear. Small's fur was muddy and his clothes were wet.

'What happened?' called Big.

'The wind blew me into the pond!' said Small, miserably, 'and I haven't got any dry clothes.'

'I've got just the outfit for you,' laughed Big. And he gave Small his tiny track suit!

BUNS

S ally Bear just loves to cook,
And sometimes she may let you look.
Today, of course, it's little buns,
You know — the very fruity ones.
They are delicious, can you see?
She's made them specially for me.
Perhaps there will be one for you,
I bet you'd like to taste them, too!

THE WALKING-STICK

'Grrr,' growled old Brian Bear into his muffler as he watched the young bears skating. 'No one wants a useless old grizzly bear like me.'

Leaning on his walking-stick, he shuffled once round the pond and was just about to head for his lonely cottage when he heard a shout. Simon Bear had fallen through a hole in the ice!

'Please help, someone,' Simon cried. But none of the other bears dared. The ice round him was so thin, if they went too near they, too, would fall in.

'Grrrr,' growled Brian, and held out his walking-stick as far as he could. Simon grabbed hold of it and Brian pulled and pulled until at last Simon was safely clear of the icy water.

Simon's family held a party in honour of Brian.

'You saved my son's life,' said Simon's father. 'How can I ever thank you enough?'

'Grrrr,' growled Brian, but this time he was smiling.

THE RUSTY RACER

Charlie had an old motor-car called 'Rusty'. It was battered and bent, but he enjoyed driving it. One day Charlie decided to enter Rusty for a race. He spent hours under the car, twiddling and fiddling with the engine.

On the day of the race Charlie drove Rusty up to the starting line. All the other cars looked very smart and shiny. They had stripes painted along their sides, and rows of sharp teeth painted on them. They looked as if they could go very fast, and made Rusty look scruffy and slow.

The marshal began the race. 'Ready, teddy, go!' he shouted. Rusty started at the back, but even though he looked scruffy he had the best engine in the competition. He overtook the other cars one by one, and crossed the finishing line first!

When they got home, Charlie cleaned and polished Rusty. And to make him look like a real champion, he painted a number one on Rusty's door, and a big winning smile across his front.

SCARECROW TED

P ut on your clean sweater and jeans,' said Ted's mother one morning. But instead, Ted put on some old clothes and a jacket with a big tear in it.

When his mother saw him she sighed and said, 'There's an old hat in the rag bag, why don't you wear that too? You'll look just like a scarecrow.'

Ted knew she was only joking but, just to be clever, he put it on and went out. He did look a fright.

As he was passing the house next door, old Mr Grizzly called out, 'Hello, Ted, you're just the bear I've been looking for. I've planted some seeds. Will you stand in my garden and stop the birds eating them?'

Ted felt very foolish, standing all morning in Mr Grizzly's garden and, eventually, he went home and changed into his clean sweater and jeans.

'What have you been doing all morning?' asked his mother.

'Scaring the crows!' said Ted.

A PRESENT FROM THE THREE BEARS

We've bought some lovely presents:
A clock that ticks and tocks,
A silver star,
A special pair,
Of multi-coloured socks,

I've put them with a message
Inside this little box:
'From Ma and Pa
And Baby Bear
To our friend, Goldilocks.'

TED AND THE VIOLIN

Ted took his violin into the park to practise. He took off his hat and began to play. He wasn't very good. In fact, he made an awful noise.

Scratch, screech, wail.

After a while some bears came up, and threw some money into his hat which had fallen off the bench.

'I'm glad you like my playing,' said Ted, and continued, louder than before.

Scratch, screech, wail.

'We're not paying you because we like your playing,' said one big bear. 'We're paying you to go to take some lessons!'

JIM'S BABY BROTHER

I've got things to do,' said Jim's mother. 'Can you keep Baby Bear happy for a while?'

'Of course I can,' said Jim. 'That's easy, really easy.'

'Thank you,' said his mother.

'Hello, Baby Bear,' Jim said in a high squeaky voice. Baby smiled for a while, then started to cry.

Jim put his paws over his eyes and played hide-and-peep. Baby looked, smiled once, then started to cry.

Jim put his arms up by his head and pointed his paws. 'Look, I'm a rabbit,' he said. Baby cried.

Jim pulled funny faces till his jaw ached. Baby smiled, then started to cry.

Jim tickled Baby under his chin. Baby cried.

Jim was fed up. This wasn't as easy as it looked. He went to find his mother.

'Er, could you keep Baby Bear happy for a while?' asked Jim. 'I've got things to do.'

And before his mother could answer, Jim was gone.

EXERCISES

Annabel Bear wanted to lose weight and get fit. So, early one morning she went to a special bears' exercise class.

She started her class by lifting some weights to exercise her paws. Then she lay on her back and pedalled in the air to exercise her legs. Finally she touched her toes to exercise her tummy.

Annabel was allowed to eat only three lettuce leaves for lunch, and then she started all over again. She jumped up and down to exercise

her ankles and swung to and fro to exercise her waist. Then she jogged around the room to exercise everything else. By the end of the day Annabel was *very* tired.

The next morning Annabel didn't turn up to her class at all. She stayed at home in bed and exercised her eyes by keeping them tightly closed. This is Annabel's favourite exercise — it's called sleeping!

TINY TED'S SHADOW

Tiny Ted couldn't find it. Where *had* it gone? It had been there a few minutes ago. He twisted and turned and looked over his shoulder but no, it wasn't there.

'What are you looking for?' called big sister Binkie.

'My shadow,' said Tiny Ted. 'I had it before I came to stand under this tree.'

'Come out into the sunshine,' laughed Binkie.

Tiny Ted ran out of the shade of the tree, and there was his shadow again.

'There it is,' said Tiny Ted. 'I thought I had lost it.'

'You silly bear,' said Binkie. 'The sun makes your shadow, so you can't lose it.'

Tiny Ted was so pleased he did a little dance and his shadow did a little dance too.

A Clever Place To Hide

When they played hide-and-seek at Biffy's Christmas party, Tiny Ted hid so well, no one could find him. They still hadn't found him when it was time to give out the prizes from the tree.

'Tiny Ted's won the prize for hide-and-seek,' said Biffy, 'but where is he?'

'I'm here,' piped up a voice, and there was Tiny Ted *on* the Christmas tree. He had climbed up and fastened himself on to look like one of the prizes.

'Well,' said Biffy, 'who would have thought of looking *there*.'

Outer-space Ted

I'm going to Mars in my space ship —
I'm off for a year and a day.
I'm all kitted out in the right kind of gear
And the seconds are ticking away.

It's all-systems-go on the launch pad,
I'll be out in space double-quick.
I am the best astrobear in the world
But I do wish I didn't feel sick!

RAG AND BONE BEAR AND THE SOFA

R ag and Bone Bear hadn't picked up much old furniture or junk that day. He only had an old sofa on his cart.

'That's not much use,' he thought.

Just then, he passed a bus-stop and saw Mrs Next-door Bear waiting.

'Are you all right?' he called.

'No, I'm not, since you ask,' said Mrs Next-door Bear. 'My back aches and my feet are killing me and I'm dying for a nice cold drink.'

'Let me give you a ride on my cart.'

Up got Mrs Next-door Bear and sat on the sofa. Her back stopped aching and her feet stopped hurting, and when they got home she gave Rag and Bone Bear a large glass of orange juice.

'That old sofa came in useful after all,' said Rag and Bone Bear.

ODD SOCKS

The twins, Bobby and Beth, were watching their mother put clean clothes into their chest of drawers. When she had finished, there were four socks left. Four odd socks — a black sock, a white sock, a grey sock and a brown sock. 'I can't find any socks to match these,' she said. 'Throw them away will you, Bobby? Odd socks are just no use at all.'

'I know what we can do with odd socks,' said Beth, and she whispered in Bobby's ear.

'That's a great idea,' said Bobby. 'Let's get started.'

Bobby and Beth took some felt and cut out different shapes — ears, noses, eyes and mouths. They glued them on to the odd socks and, before long, the black sock was a cat, the white sock was a mouse, the grey sock was a rabbit and the brown sock was a dog.

Bobby and Beth put their hands inside the odd socks. 'Look,' they said to their mother. 'We've made some sock puppets to play with!'

There is a use for odd socks!

AUNT MIMI'S GIFT

A big brown envelope dropped through the door of Jamie and Kate's house. In it was a letter from their Aunt Mimi and four packets of seeds. 'Plant the seeds outside,' Jamie read, 'and when the flowers have grown I'll come and visit.'

Jamie and Kate had their own patches of ground outside where no one else was allowed to grow things. They took their seed packets — one white and one blue each — and started to plant them.

'I'm going to make a pattern with my seeds,' said Kate. 'A secret pattern.'

'I'm going to make a pattern too,' said Jamie. 'And I'm not going to tell you what it is. You'll have to wait and see.'

Jamie and Kate knelt down back to back and carefully smoothed out the soil. Then they started to sprinkle the seeds over the soil — first the white packet, then the blue. When all the seeds were used up, they covered them with a thin layer of earth and watered them.

'Now all we have to do is wait,' said Kate.

Every day Jamie and Kate went outside to look at their seed beds. They watered the soil if it was dry.

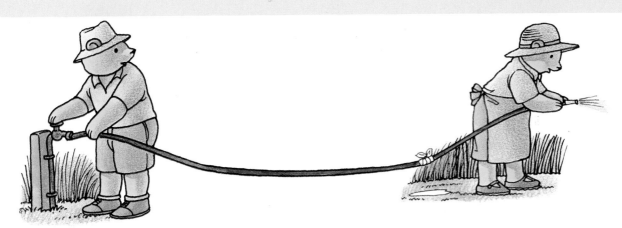

Soon, tiny green shoots started to push their way up through the soil.

Day by day the shoots grew, then small green leaves appeared. Every day the tiny plants grew stronger, with more and more leaves.

As the weeks passed the plants grew taller and taller, and quite soon small flower buds appeared at the top of each plant. The buds grew fatter and fatter until they looked as if they would burst open.

When Aunt Mimi arrived Jamie took one of her paws and Kate the other. 'The flowers opened this morning,' said Kate.

'Come and look,' said Jamie, and they led Aunt Mimi to the back of the house.

In the flower beds were two patterns, both in blue flowers on a white background. 'How lovely,' said Aunt Mimi. 'A blue J for Jamie and a blue K for Kate!'

DECORATING

I'm going to the shops to buy some paint,' said Dad. 'We're going to decorate this room.'

'What shall we do?' said Kate when Dad had gone.

'Let's do the decorating,' said Jamie. 'Dad will be pleased.'

Jamie mixed paste in a big bucket and Kate found a roll of wallpaper. She cut a long piece and Jamie slapped on lots of paste. Soon there was more paste on Kate's fur than on the wallpaper.

Kate put the paper on the wall. Instead of a smooth strip it went on in a crinkly lump.

'Maybe it will be better when it dries,' said Jamie, and stepped back. SPLOOOSH! His foot went into the bucket of paste!

Just then Dad came back. 'Look at this mess!' he said angrily. Then he saw Kate's sticky fur and Jamie's pasted foot and started to laugh. 'Now we really will have to decorate — and without any *help* from you two!'

SNOW BEAR

Bertram Bear looked out one day,
He noticed it was snowing,
'Whoopee!' he shouted loudly,
'I know where I am going!'
He ran into his garden,
You should have seen folk stare,
For pretty soon you couldn't see,
What was snow and what was bear!

THE MUDDY BOOTS

Wipe your boots!' said Mrs Bear as Little Brown Bear walked in, leaving muddy marks on the kitchen floor. His mother wiped them up.

'*You* can clean your boots,' she said. 'What a mess they're in!'

Mrs Bear went into the garden to hang up some washing. Little Brown Bear had an idea. He put his boots into the washing-machine.

When Mrs Bear saw them spinning about, she was cross and pulled them out.

'They're all wet and soapy!' she scolded. 'Why did you do that?'

'To clean them. There's not a bit of mud on my boots now!' said Little Brown Bear.

105

THE BUTTERFLY HAT

Ted put a net on the end of a stick and went into the wood to try to catch some butterflies.

The butterflies did not like this one bit and fluttered around trying to keep out of his way.

Big Bertha came for a walk in the wood. She was wearing a new hat with a big red bow on the top. She sat down on a grassy bank where Ted could not see her. All he could see was the bow on her hat.

'What a beautiful butterfly,' thought Ted.

Up he crept and, whoosh, down came his net on Big Bertha's hat.

Up jumped Bertha in an awful rage and began to chase Ted out of the wood.

Ted ran home and hid behind the door. 'Being chased isn't much fun,' he thought, and after that, he left the poor little butterflies alone.

THE WORST VOICE IN THE WORLD

The twins thought their grandad had a terrible voice. One day he told them he had entered a singing competition.

'Don't do it, Grandad,' begged the twins, but he laughed and said he was sure to win.

When the evening came, the twins sat right at the back of the hall. Some of the singers weren't very good but when it came to Grandad, the bears in the audience laughed and stamped their paws and the twins' fur turned quite pink with embarrassment.

To their amazement, at the end of the show they heard that Grandad had won first prize. It was a big box of nuts.

What Grandad hadn't told them was that the competition was to find the bear with the *worst* voice in the world.

'I told you I would win, didn't I?' laughed Grandad as he shared his prize with the twins.

THE BIRD-BEAR

I can fly!' said Roger Bear, as his friend Billy Bear arrived.

'Bet you can't!' said Billy. 'You're not a bird.'

'I'm the first bird-bear!' replied Roger. 'Watch!'

He had made two big paper wings and tied them to his arms.

'Stand by for take-off!' Roger shouted. But instead of flying, he dived straight down and almost landed on Billy.

'Never mind,' said Billy. 'Let's go camping instead.'

So the bears went to collect their camping gear.

'I'll put the tent up,' said Roger, later. But as Roger held the tent, a big gust of wind suddenly filled it like a balloon. It flew into the air and so did Roger! But he soon came to earth with a bump.

'You flew just now!' said Billy, when Roger landed.

'I don't think bears are made for flying after all!' gasped Roger.

BABY HONEY BEAR

H ave you seen Baby Honey Bear?
I have searched for him here and there,
He isn't in his cot, I'm sure,
Perhaps he is behind the door?
When I peer round, he says 'Boo'
Now that's a thing he likes to do!
But, no, he isn't there — instead,
He's hiding underneath the bed!

AUNTIE SUE'S SWEATER

I 've knitted you a sweater,' said Auntie Sue to
young Brown Bear. 'Try it on.' So he did. But it
was much too big.

Just then, his sister came into the room.

'I love that sweater!' she said.

'Try it on,' smiled Auntie Sue.

So she did. But it stretched
down to her knees.

'It's too big for you, too,'
grinned young Brown Bear.

'No, it isn't,' replied his
sister, putting on a belt. 'See?
I'll wear it as a *dress*!'

BRUNO'S SPECIAL DAY

I t was a special day for Bruno, and he wanted to share it with his friends.

He found his friend Sam. 'Shall we play cowboys?' asked Bruno.

'Can't,' said Sam. 'I'm busy today,' and he rushed off.

Bruno met Sally. 'Shall we play?' said Bruno. 'It's my...'

Before Bruno could finish, Sally shook her head. 'I'm busy,' she said. 'Bye.'

Bruno saw his friend, Ella, with a parcel. 'Where are you going?' he asked.

'I can't tell you,' said Ella. 'It's a secret.'

Bruno felt sad. None of his friends wanted to play with him. They were all going somewhere, and wouldn't tell him *where*. And on today of all days.

Bruno went home. As he opened the door he saw Sam, Sally and Ella. 'Surprise!' they shouted. 'Happy birthday, Bruno!'

'So this is where you were going,' said Bruno.

'Yes, to your birthday party!' said Sam.

BASIL'S GARDEN

B asil Bear watched his dad doing the gardening. 'What beautiful flowers,' he said.

'They're prize-winners,' replied Basil's dad. He was very proud of his garden.

'I'd like a garden, too,' said Basil.

'You can have a patch of mine,' his dad grinned. So he cut a new flower-bed in the lawn.

Then Basil worked, digging and raking it, until his back ached. Next morning, he planted some seeds. They grew into a neat row of bright flowers which stood up like soldiers.

'Look, Dad!' called Basil, excitedly. But it was a hot day and the flowers soon drooped.

'Gardens must be watered,' said his dad.

After a while, Basil was busy doing other things and forgot o tend his garden. But it kept on growing.

'You grow the best flowers around,' he told his dad a few weeks later. Then Basil glanced at his own overgrown garden. 'And I grow the best *weeds*!'

BUNTY HEARS THE SEA

Barbara went on holiday to the seaside, and while she was away she sent a lovely picture postcard to Betty. It was a view of the beach. The sea was deep blue and the waves coming on to the shore were tipped with white.

'Thank you for your picture,' said Betty when Barbara came back. 'I've never seen the sea.'

'I know,' said Barbara, 'but I've brought you a present so that you can *hear* it.'

She brought a large shell out of her bag. Betty looked surprised but, when she put it to her ear, she really thought she could hear the sea roaring, deep down inside the shell.

THE DAISY CHAINS

Barbara and Brenda were walking through a field when they saw Bertie asleep among the daisies.

'Wake up, Bertie,' they called.

'I'm not asleep,' said Bertie. 'I'm thinking.'

When the bears went past later, they saw him fast asleep again. They sat down beside him and began to make daisy chains. Soon they called, 'Wake up Bertie.'

Bertie pretended again that he hadn't been asleep at all.

'I was thinking,' he said.

'Well, look what we've done while you were deep in thought,' they said.

Bertie tried to stand up and look around, but to his surprise he couldn't; the other bears had tied him up — with daisy chains!

A Long Country Walk

W ait for me!' called Tiny Ted.
Binkie and Bertie looked round and saw their very small brother hurrying after them. They were setting off for a long country walk and had bags on their backs to carry their food and waterproof clothes.

'You can't come, Tiny Ted,' said Bertie. 'You'll get tired.'

'I won't,' said Tiny Ted. 'Look, I've got my boots and a packed lunch. Please let me come. I'll be a good bear.'

'No,' said Bertie, and Tiny Ted sat down on the floor and began to cry.

Binkie was very miserable. She wanted Tiny Ted to come too, but he only had very short legs and couldn't have kept up. Then she had an idea. She whispered to Bertie and he began taking things out of his bag and putting them into Binkie's. And guess what went into Bertie's bag? Tiny Ted!

'Hurray,' he called. 'I'm going for a long country walk, after all.'

WISE OLD BEAR LOSES HIS SPECTACLES

Wise Old Bear called to see the young bears' mother and while he was there, he lost his spectacles.

Mrs Bear was in the kitchen making a drink, so Wise Old Bear asked Binkie to look for his lost spectacles.

'I've put them down somewhere,' he said.

Binkie was too shy to tell him where they were.

In came Bertie with some nuts in a bowl.

'Have you seen my spectacles?' asked Wise Old Bear.

Bertie didn't like to tell him where they were in case it sounded impolite.

In came Mrs Bear with the drinks.

'Have you seen my spectacles?' asked Wise Old Bear.

Mrs Bear looked very flustered. She didn't want to make him look silly in front of the young bears.

In came Tiny Ted and climbed on to Wise Old Bear's knee. Then he put the spectacles back on Wise Old Bear's nose. They were sitting on his head all the time!

BUSTER'S BALLOON RIDE

Buster's auntie had given him an enormous balloon with a basket on the bottom so that he could go for rides up in the air. There was plenty of room for two bears, or even three, but Buster was very selfish and wouldn't let anyone else go with him.

He didn't mind asking for help though, and sometimes Binkie, Biffy and Bimbo would come to give him a good send-off.

One day, Binkie had asked him to take Tiny Ted for a little ride. Buster had said 'no', not very politely, and now Binkie and Tiny Ted were nowhere to be seen.

'Sulking, I suppose,' said Buster.

The basket seemed very heavy and he threw out the bags of sand that stopped him going up in the air too quickly.

Then he was off.

Slowly, slowly, the balloon rose up in the air on the end of its long rope and, just as it reached the top of the trees, Tiny Ted and Binkie crawled out from under a rug.

Buster was furious.

'Stand by below,' he yelled. 'I've got two stowaways on board.'

Bimbo and Biffy pulled him down again by the rope, and Buster made Binkie and Tiny Ted get out. He was in such a bad temper, he forgot that the basket would now be much lighter. As soon as the stowaways were out, the balloon shot up into the air.

Bimbo and Biffy were so surprised that they let go of the rope and the balloon went flying off with Buster in the basket.

'Help! Help!' he called.

Luckily for him, the basket caught in a tree and the bears were able to rescue him.

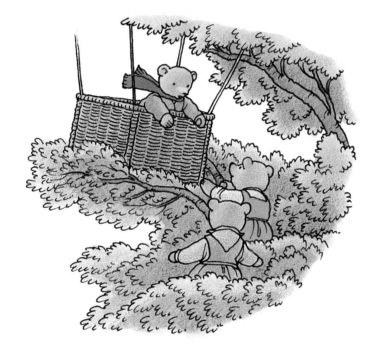

Buster was grateful and he realized that he had been very selfish.

'You can all come for balloon rides tomorrow,' said Buster, 'and Tiny Ted can be first.'

'Thank you, Buster,' said an excited Tiny Ted.

HONEY SPOTS

Little Brown Bear stood before the mirror and brushed his fur. Just then, a bee landed on the window.

'I wish *I* had nice, bright yellow stripes,' thought Little Brown Bear. Later, in the kitchen, he saw a large pot of honey.

'Mm! Delicious!' he said, picking up the pot and scooping out a pawful. Suddenly, the pot slipped and honey splashed everywhere.

'Oh, no!' groaned Little Brown Bear. Soon, his mother scolded him and sent him to wash.

'Why,' grinned Little Brown Bear as he looked in the mirror, 'now I'm brown with delicious golden *spots* all over me!'

HURLY BURLY BEAR

My name is Hurly Burly Bear,
I rush and tear just everywhere.
I really cannot stop and chat,
There is no time for doing that.
I have so much to do, you see,
And no one does it quite like me!

The Brown Bears' Barbecue

Teddy Bears *always* have picnics!' said young Brown Bear. 'Let's do something different.'

'Like have a barbecue,' his sister said.

'Good idea!' agreed Mr Brown.

'It's not,' said Mrs Brown. 'I've already made sandwiches for a picnic.' But the other Brown Bears insisted on a barbecue.

'I'll grill tomatoes, steaks, bacon and burgers,' said Mr Brown, lighting the barbecue. But the smoke got in his eyes. It made them water. It made young Brown Bear cough.

It made his sister cough.

It made Mrs Brown cross, especially when Mr Brown burnt the food black.

'The flames were too fierce. We've nothing to eat,' moaned the bears. 'What shall we do?'

'Have a picnic,' said Mrs Brown, 'like bears should. I brought the sandwiches along, just in case.'

CONTRARY TED

Tiny Ted was feeling bored.

Binkie was doing her homework and had no time to play with him.

'Go out in the garden,' she said.

But he wouldn't go in the garden.

'Don't tease the cat,' she said.

So Tiny Ted pulled pussy's tail.

Whatever Binkie told Tiny Ted to do he did just the opposite.

At last, Binkie, who now knew Tiny Ted's little ways, said, 'I don't care what you do as long as you don't play with my building bricks.'

Immediately, Tiny Ted got out the building bricks. He played happily with them all morning and Binkie did her homework in peace.

STRONG-ARM BIFFY

Biffy was showing all the other bears how strong he was. He had some very heavy weights and he lifted them up slowly and held them above his head for a minute.

'Do be careful,' called Binkie. 'You'll hurt yourself.'

'I won't,' said Biffy, and lifted an even bigger one.

This time it looked really difficult, but at last he managed to lift the weights right above his head! The other bears clapped and said he must be the strongest bear in the world.

Biffy bowed to the applause with a big grin on his face and then winked at Tiny Ted. Tiny Ted jumped off Binkie's knee and said, 'It's my turn now.'

Before Binkie could stop him he had run to the biggest weight and picked it up in one hand.

Biffy had only been pretending. The weights were made of plastic and were as light as feathers!

RAINBOW BEAR

Susie Teddy liked having her fur styled in all kinds of different ways. She could never decide which style looked best. She tried having a big red bow on top of her head. She tried making her fur curly, then fluffy, then spiky. Susie must have tried every teddy bear fashion there was.

One day Susie went to the beauty salon and had her fur washed and left straight, short and neat. But when she went home no one recognized her! Susie looked just like every other bear, and her friends had never seen her like that before!

So the next day Susie went back to the beauty salon and had her fur dyed in many different colours. After that, no one had any trouble recognizing her. Susie didn't look like any other bear — she looked more like a walking rainbow!

THE INVISIBLE MOUSE

Everywhere Tom went he was followed by a squeaky sound. He decided that it was a mouse. When he went up the stairs the squeaky mouse went too. And if he played outside the squeaky mouse always joined in.

No matter how hard he tried, Tom never saw the mouse.

Sometimes he would walk along pretending not to notice the squeak. Then he would turn around quickly to surprise it. But when he did that, the squeak always disappeared straight away.

Sometimes Tom would try to chase the squeaky mouse. But it just squeaked faster and faster, and Tom could never catch it.

The noise went away the day Tom bought some new boots and put his old shoes away in a cupboard. A few days later he realized that his friendly squeaky mouse had disappeared. It was his old shoes that had squeaked all the time, not a mouse at all!

ROGER THE PIRATE

Roger Bear loved playing pirates. He hoisted a pirate flag on the mast of his home-made raft, then set sail on the pond. Roger wore a pirate hat, cut from paper, and a cardboard cutlass in his belt. His mother had sewed him a black eye-patch.

'Avast, me hearty!' he shouted fiercely, like a real pirate. He had seen Billy Bear beside the pond.

'I'm Black Patch the pirate!' said Roger.

Billy joined in the game. 'I'm Jolly Jake, terror of the high seas,' he shouted.

'Attack!' roared Roger, bringing his boat closer. But he slipped and fell into thick, sticky mud.

'I can see why they call you Black Patch,' grinned Billy, pulling him out by his paws. 'You've got mud all over you!'

GROWL!

There was once a young bear who could not growl. He would huff, strain and puff. But the noise he made was more like 'squeak'!

'Oh, dear!' sighed the bear. 'That doesn't sound fierce, at all!'

So he went to see his dad.

'Open your mouth wider, and take a very deep breath,' said Dad. 'It's easy, really.'

All day long, the young bear tried his hardest.

'GROWWWWWWWL!' he went, at last.

'That did sound fierce!' grinned Dad.

'I know,' said the young bear, shivering. 'It even frightened *me*!'

VANITY BEAR

I think that I will never see,
A bear as beautiful as me!
Look at my ears so long and brown,
My fur is fine as thistle down.
My eyes are clear and starry-bright,
And when I roar into the night,
My voice is just the best around,
A finer bear cannot be found!

125

THE PICTURE WINDOW

When Becky Bear peered out of her bedroom window one cold morning, she couldn't see a thing! 'How odd!' she thought. 'Where has the world gone?'

Becky touched the window-pane. It was covered in frost.

'How silly of me,' she smiled. 'The window's frosted.'

'You can't go out today,' said Becky's mother, bringing in breakfast on a tray, 'you've not been well.'

'I'll do some drawing then,' said Becky. But she could not find any paper.

'I'm going shopping,' said her mother. 'I'll buy you some.'

When she came back, she handed Becky a big sketchbook.

'There,' she said. 'What have you been up to?'

'I've been drawing,' replied Becky, with a smile.

Her mother was surprised. 'But you said you had no paper,' she said.

'I didn't need any,' Becky said, pulling back the curtains. 'See? I drew a picture with my paw on the frosty window!'

ROOTIN' TOOTIN' BEAR

I'm a rootin', tootin' cowboy — from the Wild West!' boomed the bear, dressed in his ten-gallon hat, leather boots and shining spurs.

Actually, his name was Stanley and he came from Honeypot Cottage. But he did like to pretend...

'Yes, siree. Just call me "Slim"!' said Stanley, as he saw Susie Bear about to hang out her washing.

So Slim...er, Stanley... whirled a rope above his head.

'This is called a lasso, Miss Susie. Watch me spin it.'

But the rope slipped and fell over him. How Susie laughed.

Suddenly, her washing-line snapped.

'Oh, dear! I'll never get my washing dry now, unless...'

Susie had an idea. She untangled the lasso from Stanley, then tied it between two trees.

'There! It makes a perfect washing-line,' she smiled. 'Thank you, Slim.'

'Glad to be of help,' said Stanley. 'Mighty glad!'

MR GRUMPS

One day Tiny Ted saw Mr Grumps building a fence round his garden.

'What's that for?' he asked.

'To keep you young bears out,' said Mr Grumps.

The next day Mr Grumps was driving along in his truck when he saw Tiny Ted and his mother at the bus stop. They waved to him and he stopped.

'Could you give us a lift to the fair?' asked Ted.

'I suppose so,' said Mr Grumps.

He looked very grumpy as they set off but Tiny Ted and his mother were smiling happily. They hadn't gone very far when Tiny Ted said, 'Look! There are Biffy and Bimbo. Can they come too?'

'I suppose so,' grumbled Mr Grumps, and in climbed Biffy and Bimbo.

They hadn't gone much further when Tiny Ted said, 'Oh, look, there are Betty and Barbara and Bertie. Can they come too?'

'I suppose so,' grumbled Mr Grumps, and in climbed Betty and Barbara and Bertie.

They hadn't gone much further when Tiny Ted said, 'Oh look, there are Bernard and Brenda and Binkie. Can they come too?'

'I suppose so,' grumbled Mr Grumps, and in climbed Bernard and Brenda and Binkie.

When they reached the fair, out climbed Tiny Ted and his mother and Biffy and Bimbo and Betty and Barbara and Bertie and Bernard and Brenda and Binkie.

They called out 'thank you' and ran off to the fair.

'Aren't you coming, too, Mr Grumps?' asked Tiny Ted.

'I suppose so,' grumbled Mr Grumps.

Mr Grumps really enjoyed himself at the fair. He even offered the bears a ride home afterwards.

The next day, Mr Grumps was at work on his fence.

'What are you doing?' asked Tiny Ted.

'I'm pulling down my fence. I'm going to burn it.'

He made a huge bonfire and asked all the bears in the neighbourhood to come to it. Tiny Ted and his mother and Biffy and Bimbo and Betty and Barbara and Bertie and Bernard and Brenda and Binkie and many other bears came along. It was great fun.

'Are you enjoying yourself?' asked Tiny Ted's mother.

'I suppose so,' smiled Mr Grumps.

HIDE-AND-SEEK

Jake and Tim were playing hide-and-seek. 'You hide first,' said Jake. 'I'll close my eyes, count to ten, then come and look for you.'

Tim rushed off as Jake started to count. 'One, two . . .'

When he got to ten Jake opened his eyes. Tim was gone.

Jake looked in the wardrobe, but Tim wasn't there. He looked under the bed, but all he found was a pair of shoes. Then he looked in the cupboard under the stairs, but it was empty. Next Jake looked under the table — no Tim.

Jake stood at the tall window. 'Where is that bear?' he said, and he heard a soft, snuffling, trying-not-to-giggle noise beside him. He pulled back the long curtain, and there was Tim. 'Found you!' said Jake. 'Now it's my turn to hide.'

Tim closed his eyes and started to count. Before he got to three, Jake was gone.

By now, Jake knew all the best hiding places. Can you guess where he hid?

THE TARTAN RUG

Duncan's paws trembled with disappointment. His one and only Christmas present had turned out to be not a bicycle or skates or even a book or a jigsaw, but a boring old tartan rug. It was the sort of present you'd give a grandmother bear, not a seven-year-old boy bear. And his friends would make such fun of him. They always got lots of exciting Christmas presents.

'It's a special rug,' explained his mother. 'You can turn it into anything you want.'

Duncan thought. Perhaps he could. First he turned it into a tent, then into a hammock, then into a magician's cloak. Finally he imagined it was a magic carpet on which he flew to all sorts of exciting lands. And at night it kept him beautifully warm.

'What did you get for Christmas, then, Duncan?' asked his friends.

'A tent, a hammock, a magician's cloak *and* a magic carpet,' smiled Duncan. And you should have seen his friends' faces turn green with envy!

Toast for Tea

One evening when Bimbo and Biffy were sitting by their cosy fireside, Bimbo said, 'I would like some toast, but the toaster is broken.'

'There's more than one way to make toast,' said Biffy. He went into the kitchen and came back with some slices of bread and a long fork. He stuck the fork into a slice of bread and held it up before the fire. The warm glow from the fire turned the bread a lovely golden brown. It smelled delicious.

Biffy put the toasted bread on a plate, spread it with butter and gave it to Bimbo.

'Try that,' he said.

Bimbo bit into the hot buttered toast. It *was* delicious.

'Mmm,' he said. 'That was just what I wanted. How clever you are, Biffy. Now, is there anything I can do for you?'

'How about washing the dishes!' said Biffy as he made some toast for himself.

BERNARD'S BOW-TIE

B ernard wanted to tie his neck-tie in a bow like Bertie's, but Bertie wouldn't show him how it was done. First, Bernard tried himself, but it came out

wrong Then Brenda tried, but it was too loose. Biffy tried, and hit him on the chin by mistake. Brian tried, and nearly choked him.

Then Bertie realized what was wrong. He had bought a bow that was already tied, and all he had to do was clip it on to his collar!

UPSIDE-DOWN TED

U pside-down Ted
Likes to stand on his head
Especially just before tea.

An upside-down bear
With his feet in the air
Is a thing you don't often see.

My mum thinks I'm mad
And so does my dad
Because upside-down Teddy is me!

THE CLEVER CATCH

Stanley Bear sat by the river, fishing. Susie Bear came along, to show him her new hat.

'Watch me catch something for my supper,' said Stanley. Next moment, his fishing-line strained.

'It must be a big fish!' puffed Stanley, pulling hard.

'It's a big, old boot!' laughed Susie. Stanley felt silly. But he tried again. This time, he hooked out a rusty saucepan.

Just then, Susie's hat blew off and landed in the water. Carefully, Stanley caught it with his fishing-line and brought it back to the riverbank.

'Clever Stanley,' smiled Susie. 'You *have* caught something for your supper.'

'I can't eat your hat,' replied Stanley, puzzled.

'No,' said Susie. 'But for catching it, you can have supper with me.'

TEDDY BEARS' TALK

Once a year and only once,
 The Teddy Bears get together,
They have a sort of business lunch,
For bears are very clever!
They talk about lots of things,
Like berries and good honey,
And how to be more cuddly,
And what makes tickles funny!

HIGH-SPEED BEARS

Whoosh! Vroom! Swish!
 Roger Bear went everywhere at full speed on his skateboard. So did his friend Billy Bear.

Zoom!

They sped downhill and round a corner.

'Look out!' warned Arnold Bear. He nearly dropped a big box he was carrying. 'You're pests with those skateboards!' he said, crossly. 'It's hard enough carrying this box. It's heavy!'

'We'll help you,' said Roger and Billy.

They put the box across their skateboards and pushed it along easily.

'Maybe skateboards aren't so bad, after all,' grinned Arnold, happily.

IMPOSSIBLE

T homas Bear was reading to his grandfather. 'This is a long word,' said Thomas, pointing to the page. 'What does it say?'

Grandfather spelt out the word. 'I M P O S S I B L E,' he said.

'Impossible,' said Thomas. 'What does it mean?'

Grandfather thought hard. 'Impossible means something that's very, very difficult,' he said. 'Something that just can't be done.'

'Oh,' said Thomas. 'Like eating ten doughnuts all at once?'

Grandfather laughed. 'Something like that,' he said, and closed the book. 'That's enough reading for today. Come outside and help me clear the dead leaves away. We'll leave your grandmother to have her afternoon snooze.'

Grandfather gave Thomas a broom. 'Sweep the leaves off the path,' he said. 'And try not to disturb your grandmother.'

Thomas swept the leaves along the path. Rustle, rustle, crinkle, crackle went the leaves.

Thomas swept the leaves into a big, golden pile. Rustle, rustle, crinkle, crackle went the leaves.

Grandfather brought the wheelbarrow, and Thomas

picked up big armfuls of dried leaves and put them inside. Rustle, rustle, crinkle, crackle went the leaves.

Grandfather wheeled the barrow to the rubbish heap and Thomas tipped out the dried leaves. Rustle, rustle, crinkle, crackle went the leaves.

'Good,' said Grandfather. 'Let's go inside and get warmed up.'

In the kitchen Grandfather and Thomas drank mugs of hot chocolate. 'I've been thinking,' said Thomas. 'I know something that's impossible.'

'What's that?' asked Grandfather.

'It's *impossible* to collect dry leaves quietly,' said Thomas. 'No matter how hard you try, it just can't be done. They go rustle, rustle, crinkle, crackle as soon as you touch them!'

THE TWINS GO CAMPING

P lease may we go camping?' asked the twins, Bobby and Beth.

'No, you're too young,' said their mother.

Bobby and Beth looked so sad that Mrs Bear thought hard. 'Why not try *pretend* camping?' she said. 'Bring the big tablecloth and the tartan rug and I'll show you how.'

Mrs Bear threw the big tablecloth over the dining-table so that it touched the floor all round, and spread the rug under the table. 'This is your tent,' she said.

Bobby and Beth crawled inside. 'This is great,' they said. 'It's just like a real tent.'

A few minutes later the twins heard their mother's voice. 'This is a special delivery for the campers,' she said. 'Apples, orange juice and chocolate cake.'

'Great!' said the twins. 'This is even *better* than real camping!'

GHOSTS

P oppy and Sue were bored. Then Poppy had an idea for some fun.

She pulled the white sheet off her bed and put it over her head. 'Look at me, I'm a ghost!' she cried.

Then Sue put a sheet over her head. 'I'm a ghost, too,' she said. 'Let's go and surprise Mother.'

Downstairs, Poppy and Sue waved their arms and made eerie ghostly noises.

'Wheee!' said Poppy.

'Whooo!' said Sue.

'Eeeek — ghosts!' screamed their mother as she ran away to hide. But she was only pretending, and she soon came back and sent Poppy and Sue back to bed with the promise of a scary Hallowe'en bedtime story.

TEDDY BEAR'S SHADOW

H ave you seen Teddy Bear's shadow?
There — behind him — on the ground.
It never says a single word,
And it never makes a sound.
But his shadow's always with him,
Just following him around.

THE GET-WELL SNOWBEAR

One morning Ted woke up covered in spots. Dr Bear came and said he must stay away from his friends in case they turned spotty too.

What made things worse was that it was snowing, and his mother had made him promise not to get out of bed to look through the window. Ted could hear the other bears having such fun in the snow outside.

Feeling very sorry for himself, Ted covered up his head with the quilt and tried not to cry.

'Nobody cares,' he thought.

After a while, his mother came in and told him to put on his dressing gown.

'Keep very warm,' she said, 'and look through the window.'

What do you think Ted saw?

The garden was filled with his friends, and they had made him a big snowbear. Round its neck was a card, and on the card they had written 'Get Well Soon'.

Ted laughed and waved and thought, 'I should have known they wouldn't forget me.'

THE RUNAWAY BAND

There was great excitement in town. The President was coming on a visit and the town band was all ready to march past and play to him.

'Now everything is clear, I hope,' said Bandmaster Bear. 'When I say "Quick March" you start, and when I say "Halt" you stop.'

When the great day came and the President was standing on the platform, Bandmaster Bear called out 'Quick March'. Off went the band, flags flying, trumpets tootling and drums banging. On they marched until it was time to stop. But the bandmaster could not remember the right word.

He ran along beside them calling 'Stop, stop,' but they took no notice. On they marched until they were almost at the river.

'Stop, stop,' called everyone standing by. But still the band marched on.

Just as they came to the river bank, a resourceful old bear called out, 'Halt!'

And the band stopped. Just in time!

THE RAINY DAY

It was raining hard. Jamie and Kate watched as the puddles grew bigger and bigger. 'Can we go outside and splash in the puddles when the rain stops?' asked Jamie.

'Yes, if you wear boots to keep your feet dry,' said their mother.

Jamie and Kate put on their boots.

'My boots are both for left feet,' said Jamie. 'Let's swap.'

'Now I've got one boot that fits and one that's too small,' said Jamie.

Their mother came to help. She sorted out the boots, then took a thick black pen and put big Ks on Kate's boots and Js on Jamie's. 'You won't get mixed up again,' she said. 'Now go and play, before it starts to rain again!'

EARLY-MORNING TED

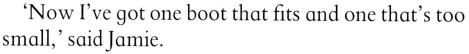

I love to scramble out of bed
Just as the day is dawning,
To watch the sky turn golden red
While other bears are yawning.
I feel as though I'm Super Ted
At that time in the morning.